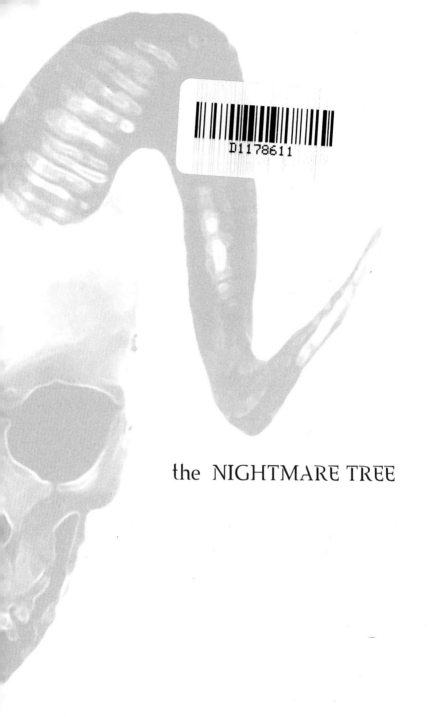

the NIGHTMARE TREE

the
NIGHTMARE
TREE

A TALE OF MYSTERION

RICHARD RENÉ

COTEAU
BOOKS
FOR KIDS

Edited by Charis Wahl.
Cover image: "Face Inside of Tree" by Brad Weinman/Veer.
Interior Djinn illustration by Duncan Campbell
Cover and book design by Duncan Campbell.
Printed and bound in Canada by Gauvin Press.

Library and Archives Canada Cataloguing in Publication

René, Richard, 1974-
    The nightmare tree / Richard René.

(The mysterion ; bk. 1)
ISBN 978-1-55050-363-0

I. Title. II. Series : René, Richard, 1974- . Mysterio ; bk. 1.

PS8635.E537N53 2007   jC813'.6   C2007-901256-6

10   9   8   7   6   5   4   3   2   1

2517 Victoria Ave
Regina, Saskatchewan
Canada   S4P 0T2

available in Canada and the US from:
Fitzhenry & Whiteside
195 Allstate Parkway
Markham, Ontario
Canada   L3R 4T8

The publisher gratefully acknowledges the financial assistance of the Saskatchewan Arts Board, the Canada Council for the Arts, the Government of Canada through the Book Publishing Industry Development Program (BPIDP), the Association for the Export of Canadian Books and the City of Regina Arts Commission, for its publishing program.

To my beloved Jaime,
And to Myrith, who inspired my journey to the Tree.

Prologue

SCHEMES BY THE FULL MOON

A bluebottle fly skimmed over an empty ocean.

He had been travelling since noon, but now, after almost twelve hours, his destination rose above the horizon like an immense bonfire on the water. Reaching the edge of the flames, the fly pushed through without being singed. Beyond, a storm assaulted him, winds tossing him around, threatening to hurl him into the black waters, until a random gust threw him forward. Suddenly, waves were breaking in an uproar of foam. An island loomed out of the darkness, and the bluebottle tumbled towards the beach.

Beyond the breakers, the air calmed to the consistency of warm mud. Ahead, the bluebottle spied the sentries slumped unconscious under the twisted mangroves at the beachhead. He considered transforming early, but decided against it. They might wake; there would be questions, and he would have to account for every wasted minute. So he spun above their heads, penetrating the thickest part of the mangrove forest before unfolding into the natural form of the Djinn – a human body with the wings of a pterodactyl and a skeletal head with spreading horns.

After dodging through the trees, he broke out into a clearing of black sand, at the centre of which glittered a pool, and beside it a great, bloated baobab tree whose branches clawed up at the clouds and the full moon. The Elder Djinn waited in the tree's shadow, hunched over in his cloak.

The Djinn landed and bowed before the Elder, pressing his horns into the sand.

"My lord," he began. "Great and high and exalted –"

"You are late! Were you seen?"

"Of course not! I got close, too, right in the tree above Mon – above his throne…"

"Perhaps he knew you were there. Perhaps he fed you some stories. After all, Malach," the Elder's voice softened, "you have never been very good at imitating bluebottles."

I do it better than you, Malach thought.

"Oh really!" the Elder snapped. "And I suppose you think you are better in other ways, too?"

Malach cursed himself for not controlling his thoughts in the Elder's presence.

"I am not the fool you think I am, Malach," the Elder said. "I will answer your insolence yet. Now, report!"

Malach repeated what he had overheard that afternoon.

"You are sure he said that?" The Elder demanded.

"Yes, Lord."

"That this boy would defeat me."

"Yes, Lord."

"Me."

"Yes."

The Elder shuffled to the edge of the pool and gazed at his dim reflection. Behind him, Malach dragged himself forward. At once the Elder turned, clutching his cloak about him.

"Not too close!"

Malach shrank away, but as soon the Elder's back was turned, Malach slithered close again, craning his neck to see around him. Dangling from the Elder Djinn's hand was a chain attached to what looked like a lump of coal. Malach stared as the Elder lowered the pendant into the water and swirled it three times before withdrawing it into his cloak.

As the ripples settled, the Djinn's reflections dissolved into another image – a boy, his eyes closed, floating on a sea so clear that his shadow could be seen on the white sandy bottom. The boy was short and wiry, with coffee skin and the face of a cherub – *his father to a tee, only much darker*, Malach thought. Then the boy opened his eyes and stood, the water lapping his shoulders. Looking into the distance, his jaw tightened, revealing stubborn lines beneath his rounded features.

Hard to pin this one down, Malach thought.

The Elder Djinn spun around.

"I thought I told you to stay back!"

"I wanted to see him," the younger Djinn whined.

"*I* want you to do as you are told!"

"He's not what I expected," Malach said, shuffling closer still.

"He is *exactly* what I expected," the Elder replied. "The old fool always prefers weakness over strength. Sending a child to defeat *me*!" He slapped at the pool and the boy's image rippled and faded.

"What will you do?" Malach asked. "The boy can't do anything. He's not even fifteen! Monvieil must be wrong…"

"Don't call him that!" the Elder shouted. "He is not your elder! *I* am your one true Elder. *He* is a tyrant!"

"Forgive me, Lord." Malach bowed his head to the ground.

"As to *him* being wrong," the Elder continued, "we must be sure. If the boy defeats me, we will be cast out again."

"You can't kill him in Lethes, you'll be vulnerable —"

"I know that!" the Elder shouted.

"Then…"

"Shut up and let me think!"

Silence fell between them. Finally, the Elder glanced at Malach and inclined his head towards the baobab tree. From somewhere in that direction came the sound of muffled screaming. The Elder smiled. "The boy probably misses his father," he murmured, glancing at the tree.

"I'm sure he does, but —" Malach sounded confused.

"So we have some incentive to bring him."

Malach scratched at his head with one long fingernail.

"And you want to be an Elder?" the Elder Djinn scoffed. "Think!"

Suddenly, Malach hopped up and down.

"I see!" he cried. "They can go into the tree together!"

"Yes, and then…"

"And when he is used up, he'll be ours!"

"Exactly," the Elder Djinn said. "Do you think you are up to the task?"

"Me?" Malach said. "I am flattered that —"

"Don't be. I just don't trust you here by yourself any more."

"I shall try to regain your trust by this, Lord." Malach bowed, trying to keep the glee out of his voice.

"You had better," the Elder Djinn replied. "Or your life will be forfeit." He shuffled to the tree. They could hear the prisoner screaming now. "You will appear to the boy in the form of his father."

"But..." Malach said, "how will I convince him? It won't make sense –"

"Use your imagination! Or would you rather I send someone else? Bagat, perhaps?"

"No, Lord!" Malach cried. "I will accomplish it, I promise!"

"Good," the Elder Djinn said. Plunging his claws into the base of the tree trunk, he tore open a large gap, and the screams assaulted them, echoing through the interior. The Djinn stepped into the tree, closing it behind them. The air inside was a soup of old sweat and sewage, but the Djinn didn't seem to notice. They descended several steps and approached the prisoner.

Malach squatted down and shook the man awake.

"Who is it?" the prisoner shouted. "Elizabeth? Is that you?"

"No," the Elder Djinn whispered. "It is I, my dear Francis."

"What do you want? Please don't hurt me!"

"Just a drop," the Elder whispered, drawing his dagger and slashing in the same motion. The two Djinn ignored Francis's scream and left the tree. Outside, the Elder smeared Malach with the prisoner's blood. Then Malach waded knee-deep into the pool. The Elder removed the pendant and draped it over the younger Djinn's neck. Malach quivered with excitement.

"Do not get too comfortable," the Elder Djinn warned. "You have no authority without my cloak."

"I know," Malach replied. "May I say the Chant now?"

"Yes. And do not return without the boy. Return alone and your life belongs to me. Do you understand?"

"Yes, yes."

"Remember your place. You are not an Elder yet."

Malach did not reply. He lifted the pendant towards the spotlight of the moon and began to chant. His body glowed red, brightening until he cried out and dissolved among the reflections in the pool.

The Elder Djinn stared down at the ripples for a while, before turning and shuffling to the tree. He leaned his horns close and nodded with satisfaction. The prisoner's screams had faded to moaning. The Elder Djinn stroked the pregnant trunk.

"Do not worry, my dear Francis," he whispered. "Your son is coming to join your dreams."

With that, he settled himself for sleep at the base of the tree, propping himself upright against the trunk, and folding his claws. Soon he was snoring hoarsely through his nose-holes.

Chapter I

THE APPARITION

J onah Comfait floated in the shallows, his eyes following gold clouds across the sky. The equatorial water
was exactly the temperature of his blood, so that he
felt the water only where it swirled around him on
the surface, rising and subsiding with the waves, or when a
current caressed his back. A monsoon breeze flowed over
his stomach, face and feet, but he could hear nothing
underwater except the mute hiss of waves on the beach.

At last he felt the air begin to cool slightly, and he
stood up. The wind had eased, but he could still hear the
coconut fronds rattling along the beach behind him. Far
ahead, the line of the reef had thickened, and Île Découvre
seemed to be retreating as the end of the day approached.
Tide's turning, Jonah thought.

Sails appeared on the horizon. *A schooner!* Pain cut
Jonah's chest as, in his mind, the *Integrity* slipped easily

among the anchored fishing pirogues, the seagoing dhows on their way to Arabia and the luxury yachts registered in Nassau. She heeled in the morning breeze, her green-and-gold pennants fluttering. The letters on her hull advertised "Hidden Islands Tours." Then she was nudging the dock. The crew hauled down the few remaining sails with a crackling sound, while Jonah's father leaned over the rail and grinned at Jonah like a pirate with new-found treasure.

A more recent memory took its place – *Integrity*, her masts stripped even of their pennants, towed into the harbour by the Coast Guard. Jonah tried to push the scene away, but it was too late. The Coast Guard captain had bowed his balding head and fingered the brim of his cap as he spoke: *We found her at the edge of the archipelago,* he had said. *The hull was abandoned, rigging a mess. It must have been driven ashore…the squall must have swept him and the tourist overboard…*

The captain had spoken to Jonah's mother in Creole, to exclude him. Just because he went to the International School, they thought he couldn't understand. *I know what you are saying,* Jonah had snapped.

Jonah, that's rude, his mother had said.

Well, I can! he had shouted. *He needn't try to hide the truth from me.*

Jonah heard the snapping of branches. His mother emerged from the trees at the head of the beach and was walking down to the water, stepping from one piece of driftwood to another to avoid thorns in the sand. Though her feet were bare, she wore the long-sleeved black dress she had put on for his father's memorial service. How straight she had sat in the pew that day, while women in flowery hats lit candles and wept theatrically, and men wearing black armbands murmured among themselves, and the mingled odour of eau de cologne, incense and sweaty bodies stifled his breathing. Jonah felt his throat closing at the memory.

As if she had heard his thoughts, his mother looked up and met his eyes. Her dark face had a muddy pallor and her almond eyes were bruised with sleeplessness. She had not cried at the funeral, nor during the endless condolences afterwards; but every night since, her soft weeping from the other side of his bedroom wall had kept Jonah awake. She wore the black dress every day.

Why does she do that? he thought angrily. *She shouldn't do that.* He tunnelled his toes into the hard-packed sand until it changed from sugary fineness to the cool gravel of broken shells and coral. *I won't get out of the water*, he resolved. *She'll have to make me do it.*

His mother was now standing with the waves breaking over her bare brown feet. She seemed smaller from this distance – girlish and lonely against the white of the beach.

"Are you coming home?"

"In a bit," Jonah replied.

"Sunset's in half an hour."

"I know. I'll be in."

Jonah excavated a shell with his toes and picked it up.

"I have something to tell you," she said. "Harry came by."

He did not reply. Harry Payet was a friend of the family. He had come back to the house after the memorial service and sat with Jonah's mother for a long time, holding her hand.

"I accepted his offer to buy the company," she said. "Debts and all."

Something gave way in Jonah's chest.

"Jonah, did you hear what I said?"

"I heard."

"We can pay off the mortgage and the bills now."

"Papa would've paid them off."

"No, Jonah." Her voice was low. "It was past that point."

Jonah turned the shell in his fingers. Then he dropped it, watching it sway down through the clear water. When it touched bottom, he shoved it into the sand with his toe.

"Payet works for the government," he said.

His mother shook her head. "Everyone works for the government now."

"Fine." Jonah turned away to look at the reef. He felt dry inside.

"Do you want us to be out on the street?" she demanded.

He did not reply.

"The bank was going to foreclose. Your father was bankrupt!"

"I know that!"

"So what did you expect me to do?" his mother cried. "Your father wouldn't sell up. He kept on saying how he would show them, he would fix everything. But it just got worse. And now it's too late, and I have to pull us out of this hole we're in! So again I ask, what did you expect me to do when someone comes along who can help?"

"I don't know!" His voice shook as he fought his tears.

"Well, I had to make some decision. Otherwise we were going to —"

Jonah ducked beneath the surface and pulled himself as far out towards the reef as he could. Only when his lungs started to hurt did he surface. The water had barely deepened – he could still touch the sand with his feet, and the reef seemed no closer. The sun had dropped behind the island. Île Découvre was now barely a smudge floating on the horizon.

The small figure of his mother was striding back towards the house. From the way she walked, quickly and with her head bowed, ignoring the thorns, he could tell that she was crying. *Perhaps Papa really is gone.* The thought slipped into his mind, and for the first time Jonah did not deny it.

Tears prickled his eyes. He wanted to break for the beach as fast as he could. Perhaps he could catch up to her before she reached the house. He could say sorry… Then he forced himself to swim back slowly, sliding into the shallows until the water no longer covered his body. He rose, dripping, and walked up the beach, leaping from branch to branch to avoid the thorns.

At the beachhead, he looked back. The sea was spilled with red and rippling with shadows. Jonah felt a weight of sadness descend on him, and he trudged back up the path that threaded through the coconut trees, breadfruit trees and scrub before scrambling to join the sea road that skirted the edge of the island.

As he walked, the forests rose to his right, tangled and impenetrable, ringing with go-away birds and crickets, to the flat granite peaks of Morne Seychellois wreathed in clouds and backlit by the setting sun.

The road was crowded with foot traffic. Gangs of fishermen in tattered shorts strode quickly past shouldering rolled-up nets. Housewives and maids hurried home, clutching striped bags or pressing packages firmly on their heads with one hand. Everyone walked in silence – none of the usual jokes from the fishermen or the shrill laughter of the women.

A hundred yards on, Jonah reached the village of Anse Aux Pins – two ramshackle *boutiques* on one side of the road and an open space of beaten sand on the other, shaded by a spreading takamaka tree. Until a few months ago, people would gather here to exchange the day's gossip before strolling home for the evening meal, but now the village was deserted. The *boutiques* had long ago closed, and Messieurs Chatterjetty and Ah-kon gone home. A bored Tanzanian militia patrol in loose-fitting fatigues now lay sprawled around the tree, their AK-47 rifles within reach. Jonah's heart beat painfully and his stomach clenched as he passed them. The soldiers had arrived, as the new President had announced over the radio, *to protect the people and the state from the enemies of the Revolution.* Even after the curfew was lifted, they stayed to patrol the streets, and people still went home before sunset.

One of the soldiers shouted something in Swahili, picked up his rifle and shook it playfully at Jonah, grinning. Jonah broke into a run, and the soldiers laughed. Once out of sight, he slowed to a walk again. *Perhaps Papa didn't go to sea at all,* he thought. *Perhaps* they *took him away, like the others…* He turned off the road and onto the gravel path leading to the house. As he passed Monsieur Malforge's place – a shack lost in overgrown banana trees – one of the windows slammed open. A shaggy head emerged.

"Better hurry home, boy!" Malforge roared. "If those demon-soldiers don't eat you up, I certainly will!"

"Yes, Bonhomme!" Jonah called, smiling lopsidedly in spite of himself. His father used to tell him that the

Bonhomme finds children who are still awake after bedtime and eats them. *Of course he does*, Jonah thought now, smiling. *And I bet he and Sungula are the best of friends too.* Those stories of the trickster rabbit brought his father's absence crashing down on him again. He hunched his shoulders and hurried on along the path that wound through the vegetation before opening up to reveal a two-storey building of white coral blocks and a corrugated roof, nestling among breadfruit trees. Lights shone through the windows, which stood open as always, covered only by net screens, so that even the slightest breeze could alleviate the sweltering heat of the day. Inside, Jonah could see his mother at the table, dinner laid out, and in spite of his resentment he wondered what she and Madame Paul had made.

He entered the house through the kitchen door and found Madame Paul at the sink, scrubbing pots. He watched her for a moment, and remembered how she had bathed him as a child while he stood in a tin basin, and how her hard brown hands had flayed his skin like sandpaper.

She looked up and her eyes widened.

"Jonah, your mother is worrying about you! Where you go to?"

"I was coming home," Jonah said. "I told her that. She didn't have to worry."

Madame Paul rested her hands on her hips. "Well she is worrying! You know what happen to people…"

"It wasn't dark yet!" Jonah protested.

Madame Paul turned back to the sink. "Well," she said in the resigned voice he knew so well, "go in then."

Jonah took a deep breath and made for the table without looking at his mother; but before he could sit, she laid down her fork and spoke:

13

"Don't you dare sit down at my table."

Jonah stopped. It was his favourite meal – dry-fried mackerel with rice and fried plantains.

"If you can't show me the respect of an adult conversation," she continued, "you can't eat my food."

Jonah's mouth flooded with saliva. "I'm sorry, Maman."

His mother was silent for a long moment, looking at him.

"All right," she sighed, gesturing to a chair. "Let's try again."

Jonah sat and looked down at his hands.

"Madame Paul!" his mother called. Madame Paul appeared in the kitchen doorway, drying her hands.

"I will clear up. You can go if you want."

"I can do it, Madame."

"No, no, you go home. It's dark and I'm worried about the patrols."

"Huh!" Madame Paul clicked her tongue. "I am just going *sur le montaigne* to get home. Those army *couyons* are never leaving the road after sunset. *Mais,* if you insist…"

"Absolutely." Jonah's mother nodded. "Go."

"*Bien. Bonsoir*, Madame! *Bonsoir*, Jonah!"

"*Bonsoir*, Madame Paul."

"'Night, Madame Paul," Jonah mumbled.

Madame Paul disappeared back into the kitchen; a minute later, the back door slammed and her reassuring footsteps lumbered away through the grass.

"I know what you think, Jonah," his mother said. "You think that because I accepted Harry's offer, I gave up on your father, I stopped loving him – and somehow, by extension, you too. Is that true?"

Jonah shrugged, but he did not look up. He felt numb.

"Now, I could just tell you that it's not true, but that wouldn't help. So I'll tell you a story. You know that your ancestor, my great-great-grandmother, came to these islands on the first ship."

Jonah nodded. He knew the story by heart.

"When she came," his mother continued, "there was no one here. It was an empty paradise and she should have been free to build a life along with the other settlers. But she and others like her were not free. The *grandblancs* who owned the plantations made them cut cinnamon bark and coconuts all day long and kept them penned up like donkeys. When she was too old to be productive, they freed her. But she and her descendants remained poor, the plantation owners made sure of that. I grew up barefoot and eating nothing but –"

"Breadfruit and fish," Jonah sighed. "I know."

His mother touched his arm.

"Yes, but listen. I met your father. He was the son of a *grandblanc*, educated by the Jesuit fathers. He had even been sent to England to attend University College and become a lawyer. But when we met, he fell in love with me, a poor black village girl from Praslin. He married me against his father's wishes. He sold his firm to buy his boat. And now I will tell you what you don't know. Your grandpapa cut him off for that."

"Cut him off?" Jonah frowned.

"His inheritance, land, everything. Your father gave it all up. For me."

Jonah felt tears gather behind his eyes.

"Then these people came, preaching freedom and equality for people like me. And what happened? They've become just another set of *grandblanc* tyrants and we are slaves all over again. Your father tried to resist what happened. The Ministry of Tourism wanted his business and he refused to sell, so they blocked and frustrated him, and he lost business to state-owned companies. That Joe Granbousse, for one, got rich on your father's suffering.

"Men were here every day with offers and threats. Your father turned them away from the door, but he had to borrow from the bank to keep the *Integrity*… In his stubbornness, he dug himself into debt, deeper and deeper. Too late, I woke up. I realized that none of his fighting was worth it. Rich or poor, *grandblanc* or not, we are all free in what we have, little or much as it is. Only what is *here* matters, what is in front of us *now*. Looking for anything else is the real slavery. I tried to explain this to your father, but he thought he could fix everything by effort. Stubborn and idealistic, just like you." She reached out and stroked Jonah's chin.

"So, do you understand? I loved your father and I still love him, wherever he is…" She took a deep breath before continuing. "But Jonah, you must listen." Jonah looked up and met her eyes. "I can't go on following this stubbornness of his. You have me and I have you and we have this place, here and now. That has to be enough. All right?"

Jonah looked down. "All right." From the corner of his eye, he saw her nod and smile.

"Good. Now our food is probably cold. Will you want to say the blessing?"

They ate and cleaned up in silence.

"And now, time for bed?" his mother asked.

"Yes. Good night," Jonah replied. He kissed her on the cheek, but he could not bring himself to look in her eyes.

"Good night, my boy."

He walked slowly upstairs, collapsed on his bed and lay there for the rest of the evening, feeling lonelier than ever.

At last, he heard his mother on the stairs and turned to face the window. He heard the door open, the rustle of her feet on the tiled floor. Then her hair brushed his cheek and he smelled the lilacs in her perfume. She kissed him and pulled the sheet over him, as she had done every night since he was very young. Her footsteps retreated, the door clicked shut, leaving only the sounds of the house cooling, the racket of crickets and the squeak of fruit bats.

Jonah lay awake for a long time, listening for his mother's weeping in the next room. He had relied on that sound to help him fall asleep. Now she was silent, and he was sleepless. He switched on his bedside lamp and read *Tintin* comics until, at last, physical exhaustion dropped him into a restless sleep.

Moonlight crept across the floor and touched the edge of Jonah's bed. Jonah tossed in his sleep, as if aware of being watched. Then the moonlight shivered and formed itself into a pale, round-faced man with dark, worried eyes.

Malach the Djinn looked down at Jonah. Ever since the Elder Djinn has assigned him this task, he had glimpsed an opportunity. Somewhere, just below the surface…

Monvieil said that this one would defeat the Elder. Only the Elder… And he was afraid too, as if the boy could really succeed… Then Malach's face broke into a smile. *If the boy is the Elder's enemy, then perhaps he may be my friend. If he does succeed, and the Elder is defeated, perhaps I can make that defeat into my victory… Make a claim…*

He worked over his plan for several minutes, testing it for flaws and finding none. He took a deep breath, leaned down and murmured into the ear of the sleeping boy: "Jonah! Son, wake up. It's me, it's Papa!"

Chapter 2
A CALL FOR HELP

Jonah struggled to the surface of sleep. He had dreamed that he was sailing his dinghy *Albatross* across a still ocean. His father had been running beside him on the water, encouraging him and offering advice – *watch the telltales, pull up a little, that's it, now tighten the sheet to compensate, that's it.* And then the boat had gone over, and Jonah was in the water, drifting down through the sunbeams towards the receding ocean floor. Beside him, his father smiled at Jonah's fear of the depths, and Jonah knew then that his father was dead in the dream too, not just in real life. Suddenly, he felt as if a claw had raked his lungs, and he knew he was drowning. He kicked and pulled himself up. But his father went on sinking, his face expressionless as he watched Jonah rise. Then Jonah broke into the air and woke in his moonlit bedroom.

Seeing the boy open his eyes, Malach drew back. A human touch could uncover his disguise. He could not risk the boy exposing his real nature.

"Papa!" Jonah murmured. "You came back up before me!"

Malach hesitated. This was not what he had expected. "Uh…" he said. "I'm sorry…"

"You came back up from under the water…"

Oh, I see, Malach thought. *He means from the dead.* He threw his arms wide. "That's right. I'm alive, my boy! And I need your help."

"I know," Jonah said, yawning.

"Know what?" Malach asked. *How on earth can he know…?*

"You want me to take care of Maman," Jonah said, and closed his eyes.

"No!" The Djinn shook his head. *This is not going the right way at all.* "Of course you should take care of her, but…" he stumbled, "I'm alive, you see…"

"She doesn't understand. She wants me to forget you."

What to say, what to say! "I'm sure she loves you."

"Maybe," Jonah said. "She just doesn't understand."

Damn! Malach thought. *He's falling asleep!* He came as close to Jonah as he dared without touching, and hissed: "Jonah! Wake up! I have something to tell you… I'm alive, son!"

"I knew you were," Jonah said. "You always were. You taught me how to sail. I loved that."

"Yes, yes," the Djinn said, shaking with impatience. "Listen, I need help!"

"I'd like to help, Papa…"

"You can!" Malach almost shouted. *At last,* he thought. *At last…*

"I could help sail your ship. But you'd never let me."

Malach's shoulders sagged. *Maybe the Elder Djinn was right about me. I'm inept.*

"You are much too young to sail my ship," he said, without thinking.

Jonah opened his eyes and sat up.

"That's not what you said! You said it was Maman who was scared of me going out!"

Malach floated backwards, surprised. *That woke him! Perhaps I'll push on this a little.* "That too," he said slowly. "But Jonah, you are only fourteen, and –"

Jonah kicked his feet in indignation. "You said that it was no different than sailing *Albatross*, only bigger."

"Except that you're on the open ocean, don't forget," Malach added. *I've got it, by the Wind! I've got it!*

"So what? I can handle it!"

"Really? You think so?"

"Of course!" Jonah slapped the sheet. "You said so too, more than once! You said it was just Maman."

"Well," Malach tilted his head. "She worries about you."

"She thinks I'm a baby and I'm not!"

The apparition of his father nodded in sympathy.

"You're grown up now."

"Yes!"

"You can make your own decisions, you can take action…"

"Of course I can!"

The Djinn chuckled to himself. *Too easy!* "Then perhaps you need to show her, Jonah."

"I want to, but I don't know how…"

Jonah twisted the sheet around his hand and looked out the window. Moonlight flickering on the water…

"Let me ask you," the Djinn said slowly. "Do you believe that I died? Do you really believe it?"

Jonah's eyes filled with tears. "No, Papa. I never believed it. Except tonight, I was starting to when Maman told me —"

"Of course she did! *She* wants to get on with her life! You can't blame her for that. But *you* don't believe it, and you can't let her change your mind. After all, what evidence does she have that you don't?"

"What do you mean?" Jonah frowned.

"She thinks I am dead. But how does she really know?"

"She doesn't, I suppose…"

"You see?" the Djinn said. "The only difference is that she doesn't believe and you do, and you need to show her that you are old enough to make up your own mind."

"But how do I do that?" Jonah said. "I can't convince her…"

"Not with words you can't," Malach shook his head. "*Actions* are all that matter in the end."

"What kind of actions?" Jonah said, leaning forward. Malach could see that he was truly awake.

This is it. Malach took a deep breath and plunged in. "Like taking *Albatross*, and coming to find me."

Jonah stared at him. "But I don't know where you went."

"You know that island that lies opposite us?"

"You mean Île Découvre."

"Yes. You know who lives there?"

Jonah nodded. "Captain Aquille. The hermit." All he knew about the captain was that two days a week a small pirogue carried a supply of tea, bread and other staples to

Île Découvre. Included in the delivery were the latest copies of *The Times of London* in plastic bags. The pilot of the boat left his delivery above the high-tide mark, and he had never seen the captain. Rumour had it that the hermit came from the mainland – Mombasa perhaps. One story even had it that he was the last living descendant of those unknown Arab sailors whose grave markers were left on the north shore long before the first settlers arrived.

"He will know how to find me," the apparition said. "Just tell him I was lost in Nihil. Then do exactly as he says…"

Jonah frowned. "How would he know? Who are you?" he demanded, blinking. "Are you real?" He reached out towards Malach, and the Djinn floated backwards out of reach.

"I'm just a dream, Jonah," he whispered. "But some dreams have meaning. Help me. Come and find me."

But Jonah was uncertain. "What shall I tell Maman?"

Malach barely restrained his impatience. "Do you need to tell her anything?"

"Well…" Jonah frowned. "She'll be upset, won't she?"

What an idiot I am. Of course she will! Think carefully now… "Yes she will," Malach said slowly. "But if you tell her, she will almost certainly stop you from going."

Jonah was silent, seeing the dilemma. "You are right. She won't believe me."

"No," the Djinn said with evident relief. "No she won't."

"But I can't just take off!" Jonah said with a note of pleading.

"Write her a note. Tell her not to worry, that you are old enough to take responsibility."

"I suppose…" Jonah whispered, looking down at his hands, as Malach delivered the *coup de grâce*.

"Jonah, one day, this will be over. We'll all be together again, just as we were."

Jonah said nothing, but tears pricked at the back of his eyes.

"You thought that would never happen, didn't you?" Malach said. "You thought I would never come back. You thought that your mother would sell *Integrity*, perhaps get married again…"

Jonah thought of Harry Payet holding his mother's hand, and he clenched his jaw.

"Well," the Djinn continued. "If you don't want that to happen, you must act now. It is a risk, but…"

"All right," Jonah whispered.

Malach smiled. *My Elder Lord, prepare for your defeat!* "Good. And remember, only the captain can guide you. Believe no one else."

"Like who?" Jonah frowned.

"Oh, no one in particular…" *So long as I can convince the Elder not to pay you a visit.*

"Goodbye, my son." Malach flickered and faded into the moonlight.

Jonah stared at the place where the apparition had stood. What had he just seen? He knew he was awake, especially towards the end, but why did Papa call himself a dream? Was it a ghost, or something else? And what and where was Nihil? And why would Captain Aquille know about it? And what if…?

So much, he thought. *So much I just don't know.* But one thing was certain — and he latched onto this thought — he could not ignore what had happened tonight, whatever it was. There was too much doubt about the fate of his father. Speaking to Captain Aquille was the only way to find out the truth. At worst, Jonah would return home to his mother's wrath.

No more thinking, he decided. *Just go.*

He got out of bed and stood listening to make sure that his mother was not still moving around in her room. But he could hear nothing but the faint tapping of the wind blowing through the coconut fronds. He pulled on a pair of shorts, the plastic sandals he used for walking out to the reef at low tide and a T-shirt.

Carefully, he opened the door and looked out onto the landing. The hall was flooded with moonlight. The air was heavy and still, as if the house was listening. Jonah went to his mother's door and leaned his head close to the keyhole. There was no light or sound within. He was about to move away when he heard a sigh. He waited, listening for movement, but none came. She was sighing in her sleep.

He tiptoed back to his bedroom. At his desk he scribbled a note in one of his school exercise books:

Dear Maman,

I know that Papa is alive and I'm going to find him. I'll be back as soon as I can. Please don't worry. I love you very much.

Jonah

He laid the note on the bed for his mother to find the next day, tiptoed downstairs and into the night. Keeping in the shadows, he ran down the path and along the sea road towards the beach.

Chapter 3
A WORD ABOUT ALBATROSS

*A*lbatross was Jonah's fourteenth birthday present. She was a twelve-foot dinghy with a single sail and a dagger-board and rudder that could be raised or lowered depending on the depth of water.

"She'll dance over the waves at the slightest provocation," Jonah's father told him, as the delivery men rolled *Albatross* off the truck. "But you'll have to watch her in a blow because she'll go over just as easily. The trick there is to keep an eye on the telltales."

"Telltales?" Jonah asked, still not quite recovered from the shock of the gift.

"I'll show you," his father assured him. "We can take her out, if you would like."

"*If* I would like?" Jonah exclaimed.

"Are you sure he's ready for this?" Jonah's mother asked.

"Of course I am, Maman!"

"We didn't talk about this, Francis," she said.

"Because I knew you would say this," Jonah's father replied, smiling. "But honestly, Liza, it's fine. I was his age when I began, in a schooner no less. This is just for messing about inside the reef…"

"Just inside!" Jonah protested.

"She's not a sea-going vessel, Jonah."

"But that'll be so boring, Papa!"

"Sailing is sailing, Jonah. Only the mood of the water changes. Be grateful. One day, you'll have the ocean, and then you'll long for the bay."

"Or dry land!" Jonah's mother said.

Jonah's father shook his head in mock exasperation. "Here, I have something for you." He held out a furled cloth.

"Your pennant!" Jonah said, dangling the green-and-gold triangle from his fingers.

"I had one made just like mine," his father said. "Yours – until you're ready to come with me."

"Huh!" Jonah's mother sniffed.

Over the following year, his father taught him all the basics:

"The most important knot a sailor can learn is the figure-of-eight bend, because you can tie two ropes together, even if they're different sizes. You take both ends…"

"The wind you feel on your face is the apparent wind. To find the real wind, look at the waves. They always move at right angles to the wind. That's how you can really know…"

"When you come about across the wind, do it firmly. Don't hesitate, don't allow her to lose momentum."

Jonah learned most about the wind – the southeast and northwest monsoons, and the in-between wind that attacked treacherously from all directions. At those times, his father taught him to rely on telltales, those threads on the sail whose movements warned of a sudden wind shift. And he learned how to capsize without falling in, perching on the gunwale as she went over, then leaping over onto the dagger-board to right her in a clatter of wet sail and rigging.

Long after his father's lessons, after his mother had given up monitoring him through binoculars, Jonah took *Albatross* out to the reef at the mouth of the bay. As he guided the dinghy to where the waves exploded against the coral, he imagined sailing on through one of the many gaps in the reef. But he always turned back towards the shelter of the bay, feeling something he would never admit to – relief at not having to meet the deep green waters yet.

In the end, sailing meant deliberate capsizes and moments of exhilaration when the wind was right and the dinghy planed. Mostly he just set the sail with the wind blowing lightly over the port side, the mainsheet tied so it would not slip, and his fingers resting on the tiller as *Albatross* cut through waves no higher than his hand. And Jonah lay with his legs propped against the hull, his head thrown back to the masthead where his father's pennant fluttered in the sun.

Chapter 4
NIGHT JOURNEY

Jonah walked quickly, keeping in the shadows cast by the roadside scrub. Suddenly, voices floated towards him from ahead. He slipped into some bushes, just in time – a militia patrol passed by. Jonah caught a glimpse of their features in the moonlight, their shapeless cloth caps, rifles slung over shoulders, and the acrid stench of old sweat and tobacco. Then, in a shower of sparks, one of the soldiers flicked his cigarette towards Jonah. The butt bounced and landed a few feet away, still glowing. One of the soldiers said something in Swahili; the others laughed. Ice water flooded Jonah's guts. Had they spotted him? But the soldiers were shuffling on in that indolent way of theirs, their shapes and voices fading at last into the night.

Jonah waited for what seemed hours before emerging. He ran the last few yards until with immense relief he recognised the rounded boulder that marked the turnoff, and scrambled down towards the beach. Between the trees, shadows criss-crossed the moonlit path, so that he stumbled several times on what was usually familiar terrain. Above him the wind tossed the treetops back and forth. Wisps of cloud scudded across the moon. It was the time between monsoons. He would have to be careful.

He saw dark, glittering water, and then the trees fell back, revealing the expanse of the bay. Loose sand spilled into his sandals and worked between his toes, but he did not take off his shoes. Those thorns really hurt.

He made his way along the beach until he came to two boulders. *Albatross* lay in the space between them, above the high-tide mark. The waves hissed less than three metres from the raised rudder. *Good,* he thought. *Full tide within the hour. The more water between the hull and the reef the better!*

Jonah wetted his finger and tested the wind. Onshore – *for the time being at least.* Quickly, he pulled the prow around until *Albatross* was facing the water. He unfurled the sail and left it flapping while he unwound the lines. A few minutes later *Albatross* bucked in the breaking waves, her sail fluttering, her rudder swinging.

Jonah dragged the dinghy into the water until the water lapped around his chest. He guided the dinghy forward, and leaped in. *Albatross* tilted dangerously, almost capsized, and then righted herself. He pushed the daggerboard down two-thirds of the way, lowered the rudder, and breathed out a sigh. Getting off the beach was always the hardest part. Now he only had to catch the wind. Carefully, he pulled the boom towards him while pushing the tiller away. The sail filled with a quiet snap; the boat sailed backward for a moment, then bore away from the wind. Jonah scrambled swiftly to port, just in time to balance her as she caught the wind, heeled and jumped forward on a port tack.

He leaned out to flatten the hull on the water and *Albatross* picked up speed. Now the waves came at regular intervals under the bow, the apparent wind blew steadily in his face, and the white sail stretched thirteen feet above him like the wing of a seagull, the green–and–gold pennant fluttering at the masthead. He was really off!

Several minutes later, still in high spirits, he approached the reef. He could already make out the white line where the waves broke against the coral and the narrow gaps where they flowed on unchecked. He drove *Albatross* forward until she was fewer than thirty metres from the reef, the waves exploding in flashes of moonlit foam, seething for a moment before roaring back into darkness. Jonah bore away from the wind, letting out the sail and lining up the dinghy's bow with a space about five feet wide. When she was in line, he levelled the helm and pulled the dagger-board all the way up. *Albatross* closed the last few metres and darted into the reef.

Then the wind changed direction. The sail fluttered, and whipped across. Jonah ducked instinctively – the solid wooden boom brushing at his hair – and threw himself to starboard – just in time. The boat rolled, then steadied and slipped through the mouth of the reef.

"Done it!" he shouted at the wind and the waves. In his excitement, he did not see the telltales fluttering backwards until it was too late. Before he could react, the wind caught the other side of the sail. The boom whipped across. He ducked, but the dinghy was already tipping and capsized over him with a loud slap.

He allowed himself to fall backwards, holding his breath as he always did when the dinghy went over. But even as he hit the water, he knew that something was wrong. He was dropping through the water too quickly. *My life jacket! I forgot it at home!* Flailing wildly, he tried to take a breath and sucked in seawater through his nose. He coughed and choked, clawed at the darkness around him, pulling and kicking against the drag of his clothes and his sandals, unable to locate the surface.

Then, when it seemed that his lungs were tearing apart, he came up under the wet sail. The dinghy was still on her side. Gasping and retching seawater, Jonah paddled out from under the sail and around the boat. The dagger-board and the rudder were still in place! Righting her and getting underway would be easy.

Jonah swam to the dagger-board, reached up and heaved down on it. Nothing happened. Feeling a slight tightening of panic in his chest, he pulled again, this time lifting himself out of the water. The board gave a little under him, and he pulled himself up once more, grabbing the gunwale with one hand as the dinghy rolled, rising towards him faster and faster until she sat upright, rocking back and forth.

He pulled himself into the dinghy and sat to catch his breath. For the first time, he became aware of the breakers rolling and tossing the hull from side to side. Hot fear flooded through him. He imagined the sea smashing the hull and dragging him down, faster and faster, as the water filled his lungs. His dinner lurched and he realized with a prick of shame that he was seasick. The clouds had reached up and concealed the moon. He could no longer see the island.

The sail luffed as the wind shifted. The boom swung in line with the stern, then into the wind. The rocking grew heavy. Slowly, Albatross drifted backwards towards the surf exploding on the reef.

Wake up! Jonah shouted to himself. He crawled aft and started to untangle the lines, costing himself precious minutes. Occasionally, the sail filled and the Albatross tilted dangerously, but swung up into the wind without capsizing.

The stern was now a mere fifteen metres away from the reef. *I could go home now*, Jonah thought wearily. *I could probably get back into bed without waking Maman... This is ridiculous! And all because a dream told you to do it? Are you crazy?*

He grasped the tiller and pulled in the mainsheet. The sail snapped full with all the force of the wind, and the dinghy slowed, stopped and began to sail forward, heeling. Jonah leaned out to counterbalance the wind, trying to flatten the hull, but it was too heavy for him. The lee rail was dragging underwater, and there was nothing he could do to right it.

I'll have to jury-rig her. With desperation clawing at his guts, he pushed the helm over and *Albatross* spun into the wind. The sail collapsed, flapping with a frenzy that filled Jonah with fear. If he could not jury-rig her, he was lost.

Jonah stood, grabbed the lower corner of the sail and unhooked it from the boom. Balancing against the wild rocking of the boat, he reached forward and started to wrap the unhooked sail around the mast – one, two, three times – to make it smaller. He then tried to hook the corner back onto the boom. But every time he tried, the sail filled and *Albatross* threatened to capsize beneath him. Finally, the boom fell off the mast into the boat, and no matter how hard he tried, Jonah could not reattach it. By this time, the boat was tossing in the backlash of the surf, and Jonah started to feel the wings of panic fluttering around his heart.

There was a grinding sound. The boat slowed and then continued to drift backwards. The rudder had brushed on coral. Without thinking, Jonah grabbed the corner of the sail, using his arm as a makeshift boom. At the same moment, he grabbed the tiller with his other hand and shoved it furiously to break *Albatross* out of the headwind. The sail caught, jerking painfully at Jonah's arm. For a second *Albatross*'s backward drift speeded up. Then, within centimetres of grounding on the reef, she spun away, heeling so that Jonah had to lean his full weight back to hold her upright. With the surf exploding over her bows, *Albatross* flew forward into open ocean. There was no turning back now.

Two hours later, Jonah's arms and legs screamed from the strain of leaning back and holding the sail, and his eyes burned from salt-water spray. His vision blurred and spun. Then his head jerked up with a start – he had fallen asleep, holding out the sail while the wind remained steady. How long had he slept? The moon had come out at last, and just ahead, no more than a kilometre away, lay the black shape of Île Découvre. At its centre shone a triangle of lights.

The pain in Jonah's limbs dissolved. He stretched the sail out as far as he could and steered for the lights. Then the faint noise of breakers floated out to him. A reef lay somewhere ahead, but he saw no breaker line.

The waves sounded louder, and he realized that the deep water must go right to the shore on this section of the island. Then the boat was rocking and tossing in the surf. Hastily, Jonah loosened the rudder so that it would come up when it hit the sand. He pulled out the dagger-board and released the sail to its wild flapping. The boat slipped in sideways on the edge of a wave and crunched onto the sand. Jonah leaped into knee-deep water, waded to the bow and dragged *Albatross* forward, pushed along by a breaking wave.

Once *Albatross* lay high on the sand, he tied the bow rope around a fallen log above the high tide mark. Only then did he rest, gasping with his back bent and hands resting on his knees. His heartbeats stabbed at him. Light and darkness flickered behind his eyes.

At last, he straightened up. He could see the top of the captain's house just beyond the high-tide line, but he had to take a deep breath to summon the resolve to start walking. After only a few feet, the scrub gave way to open sand, white as eggshell in the moonlight. On either side dense forest crowded closely. The house now revealed itself as a wooden building set on stilts with a ladder rising to the front door. A warm yellow light shone out of two large windows at the front, while a large hurricane lamp swung from the peak of the eaves.

He started up the ladder, pausing to breathe at each step. Then, with what seemed the last of his strength, he raised his hand and knocked on the door.

Chapter 5

CAPTAIN AQUILLE

As if by a sudden wind, the door swung open. There, outlined like the moon eclipsing the sun, stood a large man in a dark robe. The silver fringes on his bald head and the tired strands of his beard glinted. A distinct stillness hovered around the old man, as if he were listening to the movement of the wind.

"Now, what is a boy doing here at this hour?" he said.

All the explanations and reasons drained out of Jonah and he was left only with the old man's question. *What am I doing here?* he wondered. *I should be at home, asleep...there's school tomorrow and I didn't even do my homework...*

He opened his mouth. He had to say something. Anything.

"Ca..." he said. "Captain Aquille?"

"I am he," the old man said, raising his eyebrows. "What do you want?"

"My father..." was all Jonah could get out.

"Your father," Captain Aquille repeated. "And who is your father, and why would he let you out this late, hmm? Tell me quickly. I was just about to go to bed!"

"I'm sorry, sir," Jonah said. To his shame, he could feel tears pricking his eyes.

The captain swatted his apology away. "Don't be sorry. Just tell me why you are here, so I can get some sleep, that's all!"

Jonah took a deep breath and forced his tears back.

"My father, Francis Comfait. He's lost."

Although the old man said nothing, Jonah thought that the stillness in his face suddenly intensified.

"I heard," he said. "I couldn't come to the memorial service –"

"Yes, but he's not dead," Jonah said quickly. "He was just lost in...in Nihil."

Captain Aquille registered no surprise. "Who told you that?"

Jonah's heart thumped. *Is there something to all this?* "I saw him. I was awake, but he said he was a dream."

The old man looked away, and he was silent for so long that Jonah felt compelled to speak again.

"And...he told me that I should come to you and you would help find him."

Captain Aquille raised his eyebrows. "Oh he did, did he?"

"Yes."

"Huh," the old man said and then was silent again.

"So," Jonah asked at last, "will you?"

"Will I what?"

"Will you help me?"

"I don't know," the old man said. "First we must get certain facts quite clear. Now…" He brought his face close to Jonah's. His skin was the colour of milky tea and his eyes were both sad and smiling. "You say your father was *lost* in Nihil."

"Yes."

"Hm. That's interesting. Now, tell me, my boy, did you notice anything strange about your father's behaviour before he left? Anything he said to you or to your mother?"

"Not really…" Jonah said. "Though he did seem a little…sad."

"Oh? How?"

"The evening before," Jonah said, "me and Maman and Papa went down to the beach. We picked shells and skimmed stones. It was nice. Then we built a sandcastle and watched the tide break it down, and Papa had a sad look in his eyes. He didn't talk much on the way home."

The captain was silent. Then he nodded. "I see." He hesitated a moment before continuing. "Jonah, I have to be completely honest with you."

"Yes? What?"

"From what you have told me, I believe that your father was not lost. He went to Nihil on purpose. He entered the service of the Djinn."

Jonah shook his head. Exhaustion had filled his limbs like liquid concrete. "What do you mean?"

"You see, my boy, Nihil is the lair of the Djinn." Seeing Jonah's confusion, he explained. "The Djinn are demons. Their goal is to enslave humans. The only way to get near Nihil, let alone into it, is in the company of Djinn. They alone have access to it. No one is lost in Nihil, unless they lose their souls in Nihil. Which could well be what happened. So if your father was *lost,* he was lost in the company of a Djinn, and if he was in the company of a Djinn, he was there of his own free will. It is beyond the power of the Djinn to *force* anyone to come with them. They can only tempt people to enter their service, which they do with every trick and lie, but they cannot coerce anyone. Those who succumb to their temptation are willing."

"No, he wouldn't do that." Jonah was shaking, his hands clenched. His voice rose, quivering. "He wouldn't just leave us!"

The old man was silent.

"You don't know my father!"

Captain Aquille pursed his lips and looked away into the darkness.

"I suppose that is true!" he said. "Although I thought I did…" Then a thought seemed to occur to him. He glanced at Jonah, straightened up and patted his shoulder lightly.

"Well, my boy," he said, "I am sorry that you wasted your time coming all this way, but I'm unable to help you. The truth is, I have grown far too old for this."

"But —"

"No buts. Go home and take care of your mother. Life can be very sad. Sometimes we lose the ones we love, but if you remember someone well, that's what's important, isn't it? Now off you go…"

With that, Captain Aquille went inside and closed the door behind him. The lights went out, except for the lamp hanging from the eaves.

Jonah stood, stunned. The world began to spin, and he felt like vomiting. He stumbled down the ladder, fell on his knees and heaved a mouthful of bile onto the sand.

No, he thought. *There has to have been a mistake.* He went back to the door and knocked. "Captain Aquille. Please open the door! I need your help!"

No response. He banged harder.

"Please open the door! You must help us!"

Nothing.

A sudden fury overcame him. He screamed, beat both fists on the door. But the house remained in darkness – made darker by the lonely hurricane lamp, besieged by insects.

At last, Jonah let his hands fall to his sides, panting. He sat down on the top step, and immediately the mosquitoes descended upon him. Jonah ignored their stings. Moments later, he fell sleep, briefly starting awake only when a mosquito invaded his ear with its whining.

The air turned blue. As the sun reached over the horizon, the wind subsided. Jonah raised his head. He could see the sail of *Albatross* flapping idly, the mast tilted slightly; and from its top, the pennant dangled, fluttering occasionally like a wounded bird.

Jonah tried to stand, but pain pierced his shoulders and arms. He could barely move his arms and legs. So he sat quietly until the air warmed and he was able to stretch his limbs and massage his neck enough to turn his head. At last he turned to look behind him. The hurricane lamp seemed to glow more feebly now. Stillness had enveloped the house, as if it had been long abandoned, wrapped in silence to defend against time.

His rage had faded. He had offended the old man. Now his father was lost forever.

He thought about sailing home, to his mother's relief and fury, and the inevitable imprisonment in his room – *for the rest of the decade probably* – where he would read the books he had read so often that he did not have to think about the words, trying to imagine why his father had left them, with no intention of returning.

There had to be reasons. That was as certain as his breathing. His father would not just abandon them. Perhaps he had wanted to protect them from the Djinn. Perhaps the Djinn had threatened to do something terrible to Jonah and his mother. That had to be it!

He would take *Albatross* and continue the search without help. He could find food and shelter on the islands. Maybe he would discover the way to Nihil without a guide and find a way to rescue his father.

He shook off the fingers of self-pity that clutched at his throat and hobbled down the ladder. His mouth was gummy with salt and thirst. Perhaps there was a faucet at the back where he could get a drink before setting out.

He rounded the corner of the house and stopped. In the centre of a smooth patch of white sand stood an old-fashioned pump and a stone basin. Captain Aquille squatted beside the basin, his back to Jonah, working the handle as water splashed loudly into an enamel basin. The old man was no longer wearing his dark gown; instead, a white *kikoi* with chevron patterns encircled his waist. His bare sun-burned back was smooth and hairless. Wrinkled folds hung around his waist.

When Captain Aquille turned to go back to the house, a smile split his face. He put down the pan and waved at Jonah with both arms. "What!" he said. "Still here?" Jonah thought he heard something like relief in the old man's voice.

"There is a reason my father didn't tell us he was going." Jonah spoke as steadily as he could. *And I think I know what it is.* But something warned him not to tell the captain. He had the feeling that the old man would simply contradict him. "Anyway, I am going to find him. I came to get some water before I go."

"You are looking for a reason," the old man said. "And you may find one before you are done. However, it may not be the reason you want. Will you listen to whatever he has to say?"

"Yes."

"No matter what?"

"Yes."

Captain Aquille scrutinized Jonah. "All right," he said finally, "I will help you."

Jonah stared at him.

"But why did you refuse last night?"

"Because I wanted to know whether you truly believed what you said – and how much you want this."

"I want it," Jonah said. But even as he met the old man's eyes, he felt doubt flickering.

"Good. Your desire will be tested, believe me! But before that, how about breakfast and some rest? You won't be able to do anything with an exhausted body in the way."

"All right," Jonah said. He could not quite believe this turn of events, but he moved automatically to the wooden ladder hanging from the back door.

Captain Aquille gestured him forward. "You first, my boy." Jonah clambered up quickly, his stiffened muscles screaming. When he reached the top, Captain Aquille raised the brimming basin. "Will you hold that for me?" Jonah took the basin and the old man began to pull himself up the ladder. He stopped halfway, panting, and seemed about to drop back to the sand, when Jonah reached forward and pulled him up, gritting his teeth against the pain in his arms.

The old man leaned in the doorway, his face pale. "Thank you," he said at last. "Not as young as I was…"

How did he expect to do this on his own? Jonah wondered. Then he realized: *He didn't. He knew I would stay.*

As if he had heard the thoughts, Captain Aquille smiled and pointed. "The basin goes through the first door on your left – the kitchen."

Jonah smiled wryly, picked up the pan and strode down the narrow hallway. The kitchen had a small wood stove in the corner and a plain deal table with two chairs.

The old man told him to put the pan in the sink, then gestured at a chair. "Have a seat. I will make some breakfast."

Captain Aquille spooned loose black tea leaves into a tin kettle, added water and cooked the mixture on the stove, spooning in sugar before the water boiled. He cut four thick slices of bread and spread them with jam. They ate in silence as the morning light streamed over them from the kitchen window. Jonah had never had tea without milk or bread without butter, but he could not remember anything tasting so good.

Hungry as he was, though, he was falling asleep before he had finished his last slice.

"Eat up – you need your strength." Only when Jonah had swallowed the last crust did the old man rise from the table. "Come and rest for a while. We can talk when you have slept."

Captain Aquille led him across the hallway, into a bedroom even sparser than the kitchen. Its bare walls were stained and the only furniture was a mattress on which rested a pillow and a sheet. Thick curtains veiled the window. Jonah made out towers of books on the floor like a miniature city and a stifling smell of mouldering dust jackets.

Captain Aquille pointed to the mattress. "Make yourself comfortable there. Sleep for as long as you want."

"Thank you, sir."

"You're very welcome." Captain Aquille smiled. And suddenly, Jonah started to like him.

Jonah sat down. He kicked off his sandals and dusted the sand from his feet. The pillow smelled musty. He did not pull the sheet over him. It was too hot even for a sheet.

"Sleep well."

"Captain Aquille?"

"Yes?"

"Where is Nihil?"

"I wondered when you would ask. Nihil is in the Hidden Islands."

Jonah sat up. "That was the name of Papa's company!"

Captain Aquille nodded. "I know. When you wake up, I promise I'll explain everything. All right?"

"But –"

"Sleep, Jonah. You won't be able to think otherwise."

"All right, all right," Jonah said. Captain Aquille closed the door gently.

If he thinks I'm going to fall asleep – then unconsciousness washed over him.

Chapter 6

THE LAMP

W
hen he woke, the light had faded to grey and blue. He felt sticky with sweat, and still ached; but he could now move his limbs and head with relative ease. He stretched and, stepping carefully among the piles of books, made his way to the door. The hallway overflowed with red light from the setting sun.

A voice came from his right. "I'm in the living room, Jonah. Come and have some dinner."

Jonah made his way down the corridor and into the living room, holding up his hand to block the sun, which was setting in an explosion of colours on the ocean. The room contained a work desk spilling over with papers, more stacks of old books, and dusty towers of *The Times* teetering in the corners. Here too the walls were bare, and

Jonah had the sudden impression that Captain Aquille did not really live here.

The old man was in a rocking chair in the far corner. On a little table beside him rested two steaming bowls and glasses of some clear, glittering liquid. The old man was wearing the black robe, and Jonah thought, *He looks like some kind of monk.* The captain smiled as if he'd heard the thought and gestured to a stool.

"Have some *Bouillon Poisson.*"

The stew was spicy – Jonah coughed on the chilies – but the fish was fresh and sweet. By the time they finished eating, the sun had set and the first wave of cool evening air had washed the room. Captain Aquille wiped his mouth with a napkin, belched softly and sighed.

"As you can see, Jonah," he said, patting his paunch, "eating is one of my follies. I always resolve to eat less, but I enjoy food far too much. But you don't want to know about my struggles. You want to know how I can help you find the Hidden Islands and your father."

"Yes sir."

"Very well then. Take a look at this." And with the air of a magician presenting a new trick, he reached behind his chair and brought out a strange object. It was a lamp, though larger and more ornate than any lamp Jonah had seen. Standing as high as Captain Aquille's waist, it was metal, with a bulbous top curving to a point, like minarets in illustrations of *The Arabian Nights.* An ornate metal grill-work connected the top and the base. Captain Aquille held the lamp by a circular handle.

Captain Aquille lit a hurricane lamp hanging from the ceiling. As it began to hiss, white light filled the room. Jonah saw now that the odd lamp was made of copper or brass. He could also make out the pattern on the grill-work: around the top flew human forms surrounded with leaf-like patterns that seemed to grow from their skin. On the lower half, fishermen in boats threw nets into a sea full of fish.

"Well," Captain Aquille said. "What do you think?"

"Is it a lamp?"

"Of course it is a lamp!" Captain Aquille settled back in his chair with the air of someone about to tell a story. "A very special lamp. I was given it many years ago by Monvieil."

"Monvieil?" Jonah asked.

"I'll explain," the captain gestured reassuringly. "But before I do, you need some background. When I was a child, I had a dream. It is the first and only one I remember. I was sitting on a very calm ocean, reading a large book covered with dust and markings I could not interpret. Suddenly I saw a man with light shining through his skin walking towards me on the water. I thought I knew him. He reminded me somehow of my father. He held out a lamp so small that it fit in the palm of his hand. The man bent slowly over the lamp and blew on the wick in its centre. At once, a light that was also a wind spilled from the lamp, blowing the dust from the book and I could understand the words I was reading…"

"What did it say?"

"I don't remember." Captain Aquille shook his head. "I told my mother about the dream and she said that I would one day learn its meaning. So I forgot about it. My foster father died of smallpox a few years later, and my mother, in my early teens. I went to work as a carpenter on one of the dhows that sail from the spice gardens of India.

"On one voyage, we encountered a storm that forced us hundreds of miles off course. After three days, the crew had had enough and we drew straws to decide who should be sacrificed to the Djinn of storms. I drew the shortest straw, so they threw me overboard.

"The next thing I remember was someone grabbing hold of me and pulling me out of the ground. I remember thinking that I must have died and been buried.

"When I finally stopped coughing up sand, I looked around, but the light was so intense that I thought I had floated into the sun itself. The sand under my feet was like powdered white gold and the trees were greener than I ever imagined green could be. They held clusters of fruit like diamonds – they might actually have been diamonds, I could not tell – and in the branches were the strangest, most beautiful creatures I had ever seen. Their bodies were covered with wings, like the wings of white terns, and they spoke to one another without words…"

"What were they?"

Captain Aquille held up his hand and continued without answering.

"Then an even greater light unleashed itself in the forest. Something was floating through the trees towards me. I covered my eyes, but it didn't help. Then someone said, 'Take your hands away. I will dim the light.' I did. The light was still bright, but I could bear it. A man stood in front of me.

"I begged the man – Monvieil was his name, I found out later – I begged him to let me stay in this paradise with him, but he only said, 'You must return by your own will' and held up a lamp. I had seen it somewhere before… 'This will be your guide,' the man of light continued. 'Kindle it with a single breath from your heart and return to discover your true name.'

"I reached out to take the lamp. As soon as my fingers touched it, a great wind blew up. Monvieil, the winged creatures, the mysterious world disappeared, and I was swept back down into this world. I awoke with one arm gripping a piece of driftwood and the other wrapped around the lamp, which looked dull and ordinary. I clung there for two days until a passing dhow took me back to Zanzibar.

"I knew that no one was going to believe my story, so I kept it to myself and hid the lamp, but became its student. I studied ancient languages, mythology –"

"All these books."

"Yes. I travelled too, trying to find the magical island. I bought a ship and explored all the islands within a thousand miles of Zanzibar. Finally, I made these islands my base because they most looked like the one I had seen.

"But after twenty years, I had found nothing more than hints and shadows, like dreams that you can't quite remember in the morning." He shook his head in disbelief. "Then, one night, I had the dream, that same dream from my childhood. Again, I was sitting on the ocean, reading the indecipherable book. The man of light from the mysterious island was coming towards me on the water. But this time I recognized him. His face was mine."

"He was *you*?"

"Yes. And when I awoke, I understood why the man of light seemed so familiar in my childhood: I had dreamed about meeting my older self…"

"That's crazy," Jonah blurted, before he could stop himself.

Captain Aquille shrugged. "Probably. And I cannot explain it. But at that moment, I knew where the mysterious island was. I realized that in some inexplicable way I had *always* known, ever since my birth, and now I had rediscovered it."

Jonah leaned forward, captivated again.

"So where was it?"

"Here," the old man replied, spreading his arms.

"Among our islands?"

"Yes, and no. You see, I realized that the island I had seen was part of a world that people can only faintly remember. It's not out *there* somewhere. It's *here*, but forgotten – hidden somehow. The man of light had said *this will be your guide.* What he meant is that this lamp is the way."

Jonah scratched his head. "How?"

"It's simple. Instead of throwing light on ordinary things, the lamp reveals the Hidden Islands. The lamp's always lit, but it shines too dimly, unless you blow on it."

"That's it?" Jonah asked incredulously. "Just blow?"

"Pretty much."

"But that's easy!"

The blowing part is easy. It's *how* you blow that's difficult."

"How you blow?"

"The breath has to start in the bottom of your heart. And then, very slowly, you let it out through your lungs and your mouth. But you cannot *take* a breath."

"How long do –?"

"As long as it takes. It's different for everyone."

"But you need to breathe in."

"No. One long breath out."

49

"But that's impossible!"

"Not impossible, but it does take patience. There are some skills to acquire, but in the end, the steadiness of your will is everything – deciding that you want it more than anything. It took me many years of frustration and patience, but eventually, I was able to return to the Hidden Islands."

"What were they like?"

"I don't remember. I don't even remember leaving here, let alone coming back. And whenever I return, it's like waking up from a dream. I remember the whole thing for a few minutes and I try to hold on to the memory. I've even tried to write it down, but before I can, I forget. All I have is my original memory, and the certainty that the islands are here," he gestured. "I can't tell you anything about them, but I know they are here."

"But if you forgot everything, how did you know about the Djinn?"

"I'm not sure." The captain shrugged. "I know the Djinn are the enemy, and I know they can appear in this world. I think I was allowed to remember that so I could recognise them here."

"Why would you need to do that?"

"It took me a long time to understand, but I finally did – it was so I could tell others about the Hidden Islands. That was how I met your father." Jonah stiffened. "He was the very first person I told about the Hidden Islands. At the time he was just a boy, not much older than you are. He worked at the marina, assisting with docking ships and so on. I liked him. He had an enthusiasm about him, putting everything into whatever he was doing, whether it was scrubbing the dock or tying up a ship. That's what got me thinking that he could learn to use the lamp. I hesitated because of his age, but eventually I made the decision and hired him as a hand on my ship. I allowed him to discover the lamp and, of course, he wanted to know everything. So I began to teach him.

"We worked hard on the breathing for a long time. I think he was starting to get a little frustrated, but I didn't notice it until it was too late…" The old man's voice trailed away. He shook his head. "When it comes down to it, I'm not really sure what happened. He just lost interest all of a sudden. He started talking about pirate's treasure. I think he heard that old chestnut about Hodoul's's lost treasure from one of the fishermen, and that was the end of it…"

Jonah knew the story well. Two hundred years ago, the pirate Jacques Hodoul was hanged in the square before the entire population of the colony. Asked if he had any last words, he stepped up, raised his bushy chin and shouted, "Find my treasure, whoever is able!" According to some, he then threw out a crumpled piece of linen on which was scrawled a map to the treasure, though Jonah had often wondered how he could have done this with his hands tied.

The legend was used to lure tourists – come search for Hodoul's lost treasure! One Italian millionaire came for a vacation, and was so entranced by the story he returned two years later, convinced that the treasure was buried on Praslin Island. As far as Jonah knew, he was still excavating on the north shore, deaf to suggestions that his quest was hopeless.

"Once your father had that treasure on his brain," Captain Aquille continued, "he forgot about the lamp, the Hidden Islands, everything. He left my ship and went to work for one of those treasure-tour operators that fleece tourists. He was hoping, I suppose, to have some part of a great discovery. He eventually bought out the tour operator and ran his own business. I never heard from him again."

The old man looked down to where his folded hands rested in his lap.

"Perhaps he stopped because…" Jonah spoke after a pause. "You couldn't prove the islands exist, so…"

The captain shook his head. "I couldn't prove it in a scientific way, no. But he believed, Jonah. He believed as much as I do. He just allowed himself to let it go, as people always seem to do with things they need *trust* in. I still had hope for him, though, especially when he renamed his company 'Hidden Islands Tours.' He had not entirely forgotten, even though he had stopped believing. When you came to me, I had mixed feelings. I was afraid for him in the Djinn's hands, but I have to admit I was also pleased –"

"Pleased!" Jonah frowned. "Why?"

"Because I knew he had discovered the truth of the Hidden Islands, albeit in the worst way imaginable."

"So there is another way to get to the Hidden Islands – without the lamp."

The old man nodded grimly. "I am afraid so. The Djinn possess a magic Chant to move between the Hidden Islands and this world. They will sell it to humans, are eager to do so, but their price is a heavy one. Usually slavery. Your father paid that price in exchange for something he wanted."

"What could Papa want, though?" Jonah asked. But even as he spoke, he felt a memory stir. He could not identify it, but it left him feeling uneasy, as if somehow he knew the answer.

"Whatever it was, he was willing to pay a high price for it."

"They must have tricked him," Jonah snapped.

The captain shrugged. "Maybe. But consciously or not, he made a choice, and you will have to choose as well. The lamp is the hard way, but the only true way." The old man looked at him in silence. "Well, what is it to be?"

"But how can I choose? I don't know what the other way is like."

"And I pray you never will. Though you may be tempted to take it. All I can do is ask you to trust me and the way I am offering."

Jonah was silent for a long while. At last, he raised his eyes to meet the captain's. "I trust you. I will learn the lamp."

"Good." The captain nodded and rose to his feet. "We will begin your training tomorrow. I know it is still early, but you had better get some sleep. You will need all your strength. Use my bed."

"But what about you?"

The old man settled himself back on the cushions. "I'll nap here in my chair. I don't sleep much anymore. It reminds me too much of death."

Chapter 7

THE ELDER TAKES CHARGE

The Elder stood hunched over the pool. Behind him, crowding as close as they dared, the host of the Djinn waited restlessly, hissing and flapping their wings in excitement. As they watched, the pool distended and bulged at one edge. A moment later, it spewed out a puddle, which stretched and coalesced on the black sand until it dried into the form of Malach. The Elder waited until his subordinate had recovered his breath and made the requisite bows and praises. The host was silent now, anticipating his fury.

"Where is he?" the Elder said at last in a soft voice.

Malach did not lift his head, but carefully blanked out his thoughts to keep the Elder from guessing the truth. "He had already left to look for his father."

"Is that true? Look at me and tell me that is true."

Malach raised his head, fighting to keep his mind empty and making his eyes as disconsolate as he could.

"No, my lord," he whispered. "The truth is, I couldn't convince him."

The Elder Djinn slashed out with his claw. Malach screamed and fell face down on the sand. The host tittered in fearful excitement. All had fallen victim to the Elder's claws, but that had not dulled their enjoyment at witnessing the punishment being given.

Malach rose and stood with his head bowed.

"He probably saw through your disguise," the Elder said, nodding.

"Yes, Lord."

"That doesn't surprise me. In fact, I expected it."

"You are all-seeing, Lord."

"You had hopes of taking my place. But we can all see," the Elder looked around at the host, "that you do not possess the intellectual qualifications necessary for this position." Laughter rippled through the host. "I shall deal with the child myself. And when I return I shall deal with you."

Malach was silent.

"I have put Bagat in authority." A short and twisted young Djinn behind the Elder squirmed with delight. "He will make sure you do not get into mischief in my absence."

Malach bowed lower, his head almost touching the ground. The Elder Djinn looked down at him for a moment, satisfaction etched on his pale, bony face. Then he strode into the pool. When he was knee-deep, he turned and fixed Malach and the entire host with his stare.

"Remember, my children," he said in a whisper that carried to all of them. "I was present at the Council of

Choice, before any of you were conceived. There I was given the rule of the Shaitan, and I shall hold that rule fast unto ages of ages. Let none challenge me, as this one has," he gestured with his chin at Malach, "or they shall suffer as he undoubtedly shall."

A moment later, the Elder vanished. Malach rose, dusting his knees and dabbing at his bleeding head.

"You really got it this time, didn't you, old man?" Bagat squealed. "He's going to fix you!" The rest of the Djinn tittered.

"I don't think he will, young Bagat," Malach replied in a very clear voice. "No, I don't think so at all."

The laughter faded and the Djinn shifted uncertainly. Bagat scratched his chin and glanced around. "Trying to incite mutiny, are you? I wouldn't try it if I were you."

"I helped the boy," Malach said. "You know that Mon…that the tyrant prophesied the defeat of the Elder at his hands. I decided to help him do that. And do you know why?" There was a horrified silence. "I said, do you know why?" *This is the moment when I win or lose them.*

"No," Bagat finally whispered. "Wh…why?"

"Because if he succeeds," Malach said, "and he may, then our Elder will be destroyed, and we can be free from him at last, free to live as we want," he raised his voice, "to bow to no one and serve no one but ourselves!" The host fluttered and murmured its approbation. Only Bagat was still uncertain. Malach continued, lowering his voice. "But if the boy does not succeed, I shall take my punishment and none but me will be held responsible. The Elder will know none of this."

Bagat broke into a smile. "I think our brother Malach has a fine idea, if he can make it work!"

"I can," Malach said. "Allow me to explain."

The Djinn host hissed its approval and crowded forward to listen.

Chapter 8

SOMEONE SENT A DREAM

At daybreak, Jonah's mother Elizabeth looked out to sea, as if she could hear something just beyond the horizon.

She heard a crackling and turned. A balding, pear-shaped man was approaching over the fallen coconut fronds. He wore white linen pants and a white short-sleeved shirt, his peaked cap tucked under his arm.

Monsieur Joubert, Captain of the Coast Guard, pulled out a handkerchief and mopped the rivers of sweat running down his forehead. Finally, he tucked the handkerchief away and wiped a hand back over his hair to smoothe it.

They stood in silence for several minutes.

"The bishop sends his regards," he said at last.

"You met him?" Elizabeth asked without turning her eyes from the horizon.

"He was blessing a boat at the dock."

"Oh." She glanced sideways. "That's all he said?"

The captain hesitated. "He also said that he's willing to hold a service for your son whenever –"

Elizabeth Comfait shook her head. "Not yet."

The captain was silent. "It's been three –"

"I know how long it's been."

"And you know that I will search as long as is necessary."

"It's all right, Monsieur Joubert." She turned and he was disturbed by the calm in her eyes.

"You mean…call it off?"

"Yes."

"I don't understand."

"In a month," she said. "Tell the bishop."

"In a month what?"

"If they are not back in a month, then we can hold a service."

"They?" Monsieur Joubert frowned. "You mean Jonah."

"No." She held his gaze. "I meant *they*."

Monsieur Joubert shook his head. "Francis too?"

"Yes."

There was no trace of weeping in her heart-shaped face. The morning sun rising from the sea lit up her features.

"How do you know?" he asked.

Elizabeth turned her eyes back to the horizon.

"Because someone sent a dream," she said.

Chapter 9

THE EASIER WAY

J onah sat in Captain Aquille's kitchen, looking down into his teacup. The lamp stood on the table beside him, glinting in the morning light.

"I dreamed about my father last night," he said.

"Oh yes?" Captain Aquille sipped his tea.

"He was hanging from a tree, and when I called for him to come down, he said, 'Don't pick me. I'm not ripe yet.' And you were there too," Jonah glanced at Captain Aquille. "I asked you for help but you pointed down and I saw that you didn't have legs. I screamed at you and the dream ended."

"Screamed, eh?" Captain Aquille said, raising his eyebrows.

"Yes, I was screaming because you didn't help him."

"But I didn't have any legs," the old man pointed out, smiling.

"I didn't care about that," Jonah insisted. "I just wanted you to save him."

"Calm down. I was joking," Captain Aquille said. "It was just a dream. I am with you now, and I will do everything I can to help. Let your nightmare go."

"All right…" Jonah said, chewing on toast that tasted like sawdust. He had not been hungry for days.

Captain Aquille put his hand on Jonah's shoulder.

"I realize the practising has been difficult, but –"

"I know," Jonah said, shrugging his hand off. "I just have to keep trying. What I don't understand is why it has to be so difficult. I mean, just lighting a lamp!"

"It's worth it. That's all I can say."

"Well, maybe I don't believe in this as much as I thought," Jonah said in a low voice.

The old man looked down and nodded. "Perhaps you are right."

Jonah felt his heart grow heavy inside him. *He wasn't supposed to say that.* "It's just that," he said, trying somehow to excuse what he had said, "I can't stand the thought of Papa, alive, but I can't get to him because I won't try."

"I know, Jonah."

"Maybe I'm just tired. I can be tired, can't I?"

"Of course." Captain Aquille was silent for a moment. "Maybe it is time to take a break," he said at last. "There's a good beach on the other side of my island. Go swimming. Then decide what you want to do."

"But I don't want to give up!"

"I'm not suggesting that. But perhaps you need clarity – and focus."

"But how will *swimming* help?"

"It's amazing what some time alone will do for you," the old man said, looking at his hands. "Trust me, it will help. Go on and enjoy yourself. We'll practise tomorrow."

Jonah shrugged. Despite the captain's assurances, heaviness filled his body. "Fine. Should I take the lamp?"

"The lamp is yours unless you give it up. Until then, you must carry it with you."

"I'll see you later, then."

"Right ho," Captain Aquille said, and Jonah noticed a distinct sadness in his voice.

Jonah swam the warm, shallow waters inside the reef, diving to the bottom, then floating on the surface and looking up at the clouds that rolled high above him in immense thunderheads.

At noon, he sat in the shade of a coconut tree and tried to eat the sandwich he had packed, but activity hadn't coaxed his hunger back. He just sat, staring out at the reef and an ocean that glittered like polished emeralds.

Nothing's changed, he thought. *Here I am, sitting and waiting, and Papa is out there somewhere.* He glanced down to where the lamp lay gleaming beside him. *What's the use of that thing? Maybe the captain's crazy, maybe he dreamed it all.*

Several feet away, a dust devil kicked up sand and dry leaves. Jonah watched it, still buried in his thoughts. *Maybe I should just get going, stop relying on the old man. He can't prove anything...*

The dust devil darted towards Jonah. He broke off his thoughts and held up his hand, squinting as the sand flew into his eyes. Leaves and sand stung his arms and legs. When the wind died, Jonah opened his eyes. Before him stood a very tall man in a linen suit with a black shirt buttoned to the neck, like a priest without a collar. His bald face resembled meat left too long in the refrigerator, his eyes lurked deep in their sockets.

"I am glad to meet you, Master Jonah. My name is Mr. Geist."

"Where did you come from?" Jonah asked as he scrambled to his feet.

"I have been hiding. Like a fly on a wall."

"What do you want from me?"

"I want nothing from you," Mr. Geist replied. "The question is, what do you want from *me*?"

Jonah frowned. "I don't even know you."

"Actually, you do know me, if only vicariously."

"What do you mean?"

Mr Geist inclined his head. "Do you recognise this?"

He held out a scrap of green-and-gold cloth. Jonah's heart beat painfully in his chest. "The pennant from Papa's ship," he whispered at last.

"Yes," Mr. Geist smiled. "I was the tourist who accompanied him on his last voyage."

"And now you're here." Jonah's mind spun.

"Aquille must have told you – I come and go as I please."

With a shock, Jonah understood. "You're a Djinn."

"Congratulations!" Mr. Geist said, clapping his hands politely.

"Where is he?"

"Your father wanted something and I gave it to him," the Djinn replied. "Now he is in my service, and will remain there until his debt is paid. So the question is, what will you do to free him?"

"Anything."

"Really? Willingness is willingness, no matter what the endeavour. Yet you hardly seem committed to this one –" he gestured at the lamp, "– though I admit it is useless."

"I told you, I'll do anything."

"Would you serve me to earn your father's freedom?"

Jonah stared at the Djinn.

"You mean, buy your Chant?" he said.

"You know about it. Good for the old man. Yes, would you buy the Chant?"

"But that doesn't make any sense." Jonah frowned. "Say I bought the Chant and had to become your slave as payment. Why would you release my father? You wouldn't have to!"

Mr. Geist raised his eyebrows. "Clever boy. And you would be right, under ordinary circumstances. However, these are not ordinary circumstances. You see, you are a valuable commodity in the Hidden Islands. Certain people who consider themselves very important there have placed a rather large value on you. You are worth more to them, and me, than the mere price of the Chant. You are also worth your father's freedom. All you have to do is take this and the contract will be made." Mr. Geist reached into his jacket pocket and pulled out a dark, shapeless stone attached to a chain. He held it out towards Jonah. "You will see your father today, and he will be free."

Jonah stared at the stone. At first, he thought it was a lump of coal. But the more he looked, the duller the surface appeared. An itch of frustrated curiosity crept over him. *It would be so easy*, he thought. *I could free Papa right now, and not have to worry about lamps and breathing out without stopping and…* He felt his hand trying to move forward, and it was only with some effort that he kept it still. Somehow he knew that there would be no going back. His father would be free, but he would be lost. He would never see either of his parents again.

He needed time to think.

"So," he said, glancing up at Geist, "this will work better than the lamp?"

"Instantaneously," the Djinn replied. "You can spend the next twenty years trying to make that lamp work, or you can have the Hidden Islands now. It is your choice."

Geist glanced away, as if he was not interested in Jonah's reply, but Jonah could see the Djinn watching from the corner of his eye. That small deception made Jonah hesitate.

"And how long will I have to serve you?"

The Djinn's eyes darted back. "Until your debt is paid," he said, smiling at his own wit.

A voice, hoarse and exhausted, interrupted.

"Why don't you tell him the truth?"

Captain Aquille stood several feet away, half-concealed by the trees. He was clutching his left arm, his face grey and dripping with sweat.

"He is perfectly capable of making his own decision," Geist said. The pendant had disappeared and Geist now rested his hand in his pocket. He was shaking, as if in the grip of some strong emotion.

"I agree," Captain Aquille replied, panting. "But only when he has been given accurate information on which to base it. On that score, I don't think you've been much help."

Jonah looked back and forth between them, speechless.

"You know that I must stay within certain boundaries," Geist said in a tight voice, "and I have." He seemed even paler than before – if that was possible – and his shaking had intensified.

"But you have omitted certain details," the captain said. "Such as the fact that he would probably not return when you were done with him."

At that moment, Geist leapt at the captain with his pale, claw-like hands extended.

"Captain!" Jonah screamed. But the old man simply stopped speaking and spread his arms. Geist hit his chest with both hands. As he did so, something extraordinary happened. The Djinn swelled, his clothes tearing and falling away as his arms bulged with muscles, and ox-like horns spread from the side of his head. Only his face retained the same shape and expression, though his skin darkened from ice white to the colour of fresh blood.

"Damn you!" Geist whispered. "You exposed me!"

Collapsed at his feet, Captain Aquille groaned in anguish. A moment later, the sunlight around him flickered, and came back again. At the same time, a rumbling began, accompanied by an earth tremor that shook the trees and threw Jonah to the ground.

A sudden rage swept over Jonah. He launched himself forward. He knew it was hopeless, for the Djinn was twice as tall as he was, and muscular, but he did not care.

"Listen to reason, boy!" the Djinn yelled, raising a hand. "You can have everything! Don't throw this chance away!"

Instead, Jonah swung his whole body into the hardest punch he could. The Djinn swore viciously and spun like a top. At once a dust devil roared up, obscuring the sun, throwing sand in Jonah's eyes so that he stumbled to a halt. As suddenly as it had arisen, the dust devil stopped. For a moment afterwards a cloud of dust hung in the air, then slowly dissipated. Geist had vanished.

"That was a dangerous thing to do." The faint, ragged voice of Captain Aquille spoke. He was clutching at his chest and panting with the pain. "My heart. The Djinn used his magic to stop it for a moment."

Jonah knelt down beside him. "Why did you let him do that?"

"It was the only way I could help you believe. Jonah, you are no longer safe here. I cannot protect you here, only in the Hidden Islands. There I can help you. You must reveal the islands. Kindle the lamp."

"But…" Jonah stuttered. "How…?"

"I will help you. Go on. Get it."

Jonah ran to get the lamp. As he squatted again beside the captain, his hands shook.

"Lower," Captain Aquille whispered. He raised himself, muscles quivering.

"Captain?"

"It's fine, it's fine. Lower your head…so your eyes are level with the wick." Jonah did so, crouching uncomfortably until he could see through the ornate grillwork of the lamp to Captain Aquille's pain-dilated eyes.

"Now blow."

"Wait. What will happen to you? Will you come with me?"

"I will be with you. I have finished what I have to do here."

"What do you mean…? Are you sure?"

"Yes. Now kindle the lamp."

Jonah focused and blew slowly into the lamp without taking an inward breath – as he had practised.

Perhaps the intensity of the old man's pain washed away all distractions, but as soon as Jonah began to blow, a tiny flame flickered to life in the very centre of the lamp. He blinked in surprise. Then the air in his lungs grew thin, the flow of air from his lips faded, and the flame began to flicker.

"Jonah!" Captain Aquille shouted with surprising strength. "Look at me!"

Jonah met the old man's gaze. He continued blowing, feeling a pain in his chest, spreading until it was burning through him. Dizzy, he steadied himself on his hands and continued to stare into Captain Aquille's eyes. The lamp was as bright as a bulb now, and still he continued blowing, not knowing where the breath was coming from, for his lungs had emptied long ago. Around him the island darkened, as if the moon was eclipsing the sun. Only the eyes of Captain Aquille and the flame of the lamp remained.

And still the lamp flared brighter.

Then suddenly, the light that flowed from Captain Aquille's eyes exploded to cover everything in a sheet of fire. Jonah felt himself dissolve into his breathing, unable to stop exhaling. The island stretched and dropped below him. For an instant the clouds and air and sunlight flashed down past him, and then they too vanished as he was swept upwards and upwards into a river of pure, endless light.

Chapter 10
THE TRAP IS SET

The shapeless form of the Elder Djinn slid out of the pool beside the Nightmare Tree and began to congeal on the sand. The Djinn flapped down from the stunted trees that edged the clearing and crowded towards him, eager to hear what had happened.

"The first to come within arm's reach will lose his head!" the Elder shouted. The host shrank back, waiting in fearful silence until the Elder had finally hardened into his natural form, then bowed to the ground.

The Elder stared at them balefully. Malach laughed to himself. *He's trying to think of a way to explain his failure.* Then the Elder spoke: "The boy will try to come here on his own," he said. "All we need to do is guide him and he will be ours."

No one spoke.

"Bagat!" the Elder shouted. The younger Djinn shuffled out of the crowd on his knees, his head still bowed. "Stand up!" the Elder growled. Bagat rose to his feet but kept his head down.

"I am here, my lord," he murmured.

"You will guide the boy here safely."

Bagat's eyes grew wide. "My lord! I am honoured…"

"Shut up! Make sure he is alone or our plans may be complicated. Do not make yourself known or the tyrant may guess our plan. Go immediately!"

Without another word, the Elder turned and stalked away. Once he had disappeared through the twisted black trees of the forest, Malach gestured to Bagat, who sidled up, trying to look casual.

You know what to do? Malach spoke into Bagat's mind. Bagat's eyes widened and looked around as if wondering where the voice was coming from. Then he looked at Malach with open awe.

"You have the power!"

"Of course, my boy," Malach replied, casually lowering his head and stroking his horns. "All who wish to be Elder must possess it. Geist does not know of my abilities. But he will learn."

"Teach me too."

"In time, in time," Malach patted his shoulder. "I will see how you do with our task and then decide."

"I will not disappoint you, Master," Bagat declared.

"It's a noble task, Bagat." Malach looked at him intently, a fervent light in his red eyes. "This is no mere adventure. It could cost your life."

"I am ready," Bagat whispered, shivering with awe.

"Freedom, Bagat," Malach hissed. "Do you know what that means? Freedom for me, for you and for our brothers." He cast a venomous gaze around the trees where the Djinn host roosted, hissing among themselves. "Freedom from this!

"We were not made to be slaves. We were not made to squat on the edge of the tyrant's world and wait for a senile old fool to gratify his ego at our expense. We were made to conquer and live at our own pleasure, calling one another 'friend' and 'brother'…"

"Yes, Master!"

"Shh!" Malach said, looking around, while noting Bagat's deference. "Do you want to betray us?"

"Sorry, Master," Bagat muttered, lowering his head.

"Now do as you were asked. At the right moment, I will signal and you will act…"

"I will, Master."

"Go then." Malach gestured him away and immersed himself in an inspection of his claws. Bagat collapsed into a bluebottle fly and darted into the dark sky.

Chapter II

UNBURIED IN MYSTERION

J onah could feel nothing through his body. Only his consciousness floated up the river of light.

After an unknown time, the river slowed. Jonah felt his limbs coalesce suddenly – a molten fluid thickening into something like wet clay. Then, suddenly, he was encased in solid earth. Sand filled his mouth and his throat burned. He tried to move but his body was fixed in place by the earth around him. He screamed, but no sound emerged. Instead, he sucked soil into his lungs. His consciousness faded.

Then, dimly, he heard digging. The weight of the earth lightened and loosened. Jonah clawed weakly, gaining some movement, just as someone reached through the remaining soil, grabbed him under his armpits and dragged him out.

He lay for a while on the ground, coughing up sand in painful gasps. The air was warm and soft and somehow comforting, although he heard nothing. Perhaps the sand had filled his ears.

His breathing finally eased, though his lungs still burned with a fire that brought on an occasional coughing fit. He cleared out his eyes and ears, sat up to look around and immediately squinted again. Before him stood a tall, bright figure exploding with light. The being seemed to flicker, and its movement suggested that it was floating. Beyond the figure, Jonah was aware of trees and darkness, but the brightness of the light and his own blurry vision obscured the details. He rubbed his eyes, and concentrated. The person came into focus – a tall, athletic girl hovered one foot above the ground. Her body was covered by wings.

"Are you an angel?"

"Not like you think!" the girl declared. "I am an Angelus. And there's a big difference, I can tell you! We aren't human beings with wings. And we just look male and female for your sake."

A fit of coughing seized Jonah and he bent over double until it passed.

"Where am I?" He whispered at last.

"This is Mysterion. And you are welcome, young Letheis."

"My name is Jonah."

"I'm Azrel," the Angelus said. "And get it straight – any smart remarks like 'just like a girl' and I will tickle you to death with my feathers!"

At first surprised, Jonah rose to the challenge.

"So defensive," he said, grinning. "Just like a girl."

Azrel laughed.

"Very good!" she cried. "For something I dug up, you have personality."

"Just you wait," Jonah replied.

"I'll try to contain myself," Azrel laughed. "But now," she grew serious, "we need to get to Monvieil."

"Monvieil..." Jonah's eyes widened. "The man of light from Captain Aquille's story!"

"I've never heard him called that before," Azrel said. "But I suppose it makes sense. He rules Mysterion." ·

Jonah frowned and shook his head.

"The Hidden Islands." Azrel sighed deeply. "That's what he calls them in Lethes, and –"

"Lethes?"

Azrel threw up her hands. "He'll tell you everything when you meet him." She looked up at the sky, and Jonah followed her glance towards the moon, which was larger than he had ever seen it. "In fact," the Angelus said, "we were supposed to be there ten minutes ago, so we'd better get going."

Jonah struggled to his feet and tried to balance, but his legs were so rubbery that they almost landed him back on the sand. By the time he got his footing, Azrel was nothing more than a moving light among the dark trees.

"Wait!" Jonah shouted, panicking.

The light brightened. Azrel reappeared. "What's your problem? Why are you dawdling? Hurry up!"

"In case you didn't notice, I don't have wings," Jonah said. "Poor human being that I am, stuck with legs –"

"How old are you?"

"Fourteen."

"Well you move like someone seven times your age."

Jonah shrugged. "Perhaps the weight of my intelligence is slowing me down."

"Ha ha," Azrel rolled her eyes in mock despair. "Well," she sighed. "Excuses aside, I forgot that you Letheis are always rather weak-kneed when you are first unburied. I'll carry you. Get on."

Jonah hesitated.

"What are you waiting for? Get on!"

Jonah came up behind her and gripped her shoulders. The feathers of her skin shivered softly, like handfuls of living birds. He hopped up, feeling foolish and awkward to have his legs wrapped around her fluttering waist.

"Ugh!" Azrel groaned. "You only look like a shrimp!"

"Muscle weighs more than fat."

Azrel laughed. "Too bad your mouth is faster than your body."

As they floated above the treeline, the darkness of the island seemed dotted with burning trees.

"What's wrong?" he said, pointing with his free arm.

"Nothing's wrong. They're Angeli," Azrel replied. "We come from Angeli Island at sunset to guard Monvieil's people from Djinn or pirates. We call ourselves the Night lights." She laughed at her joke.

"You have pirates here?"

"There are many things here," Azrel said. "You'll learn."

She moved towards a range of mountains that ran down the centre of the island. As they ascended, the lit trees grew sparser, until the darkness was unremitting.

"We're nearly there."

"I don't see anything."

"Of course you don't. Monvieil doesn't need a night light."

Azrel plunged so quickly that Jonah's heart rose into his mouth. A moment later, Azrel slowed to a stop.

"Off you get." Jonah slid a few feet to the ground, his legs collapsing under him.

"Thanks," he said. "You could have landed, you know."

"Angeli never touch the ground with their feet," Azrel said with a shrug. "It's considered rude."

Jonah stood and dusted off his shorts. The frustrating thing about this Angelus, he thought, was that there was nothing really wrong with her. She was just so, well, *irritating.*

"Where's Monvieil?"

"Over there," Azrel said pointing into the darkness. "Follow me." She somehow dimmed her skin until she was barely visible and Jonah hobbled behind her. They seemed to be walking over a plateau, for the ground was no longer rising and he could make out the darker outline of the mountains against the sky.

Azrel stopped and raised her arm. Light flooded the plateau. Jonah narrowed his eyes and looked through his fingers. He just made out a solid rank of silver-winged Angeli, each one holding two scimitars crossed on its chest. The line formed a protective guard around a dome of darkness within.

"The garden of Monvieil," Azrel said softly.

She nodded at the Angeli, who immediately opened a space through which Azrel floated. Jonah hesitated. His legs were shaking still, but no longer from weakness. He could feel his heart throwing itself against his ribs like a trapped creature.

"Come on, Jonah."

For some reason, the sound of his name on Azrel's lips gave him confidence, and he stepped forward through the line of Angeli. They kept their eyes fixed forward, and closed ranks silently behind him.

Jonah found himself in a small, bright garden. Above, he could see the night sky filled with stars, but the garden was illumined by an afternoon light that radiated from its trees and bushes and even from the ground itself. Some of the trees were familiar, slender ones carrying bunches of bananas or clusters of coconuts, spreading trees thick with golden-apples or mangoes. Others, however, had leaves so green that his eyes hurt to look at them and branches hung with immense diamonds, emeralds and sapphires. Beneath them herds of unicorns stretched their necks to graze on the gems, but galloped away as he approached.

"They're still shy of human beings," Azrel said. "From the dark times."

Jonah stood beneath the Jewel trees, longing to reach up and pick one, just to see what it felt like in his hand.

"Once upon a time, this was the food of all the People of the Wind, but only the unicorns know how to eat them now. Perhaps one day, we will all remember again."

Jonah noticed thick bushes growing around each tree, clustered with berries like miniature bulbs.

"Bright fruit," Azrel said. "They're our consolation. They gain their taste from the Jewel trees. Try one."

The berries were warm to Jonah's touch, and he gasped as they exploded sweet and sour in his mouth. All his weariness fell away.

"Not a bad consolation, eh?"

"If *these* taste this good," Jonah said, "imagine what the Jewels —"

"Don't." Azrel closed her eyes with a pained expression. "Don't torment me."

As they walked deeper into the garden, the bushes gave way to a series of pools with narrow, grassy paths between them.

"Seeing Pools," Azrel said. "You can see all Mysterion in them, if you look long enough."

Jonah walked carefully along the paths, looking into the pools.

In one Jonah saw mermaids with hand-held nets herding shoals of fish across a seaweed plain; in another, fauns and satyrs and fairies danced by night to the music of the panpipe, cymbal and drum. Each pool held a different wonder:

Men and women with swords descended from the skies on the backs of Angeli as a fleet of dhows and square-riggers flying the skull and crossbones fired their cannon against them; a Cyclops dozed under a coconut tree, the only vegetation of a rocky island; the phoenix exploded in a cloud of flame before rising from its own ashes with bronze wings spread; a dragon frolicked in the ocean, turning somersaults in the air before landing in an explosion of water; Angeli fought a pitched battle in mid-air against an attacking swarm of winged, skeletal creatures.

Hundreds of other sights were too far away to see.

A deep, familiar voice called. "You could spend your whole life looking and never see it all."

Jason looked up. Ahead of him the pools came to an end, opening into a small clearing covered with carpet-grass. The air was filled with butterflies with the faces of children that gathered around Jonah in colourful clouds, calling to one another in high voices.

"Off you go, little ones," the voice said. "Let Master Jonah come in peace."

The butterfly children scattered to engage in a game of complicated acrobatics. Jonah now saw that Azrel had floated to a golden-apple tree at the centre of the clearing, and was standing at attention beside a silver couch. Lying there was an old man.

"Captain Aquille!" Jonah ran forward – and skidded to a halt as a black-maned lion leapt to its feet behind the couch and ran around to place itself in front of the old man, its mane bristling and growls rumbling in its throat.

"It's all right, Nicholas," Captain Aquille said. "We were expecting him."

The lion let out a rumble.

"Because you were asleep when we discussed it."

The lion snorted loudly and tossed his mane.

"Well, you'll have to trust me on this, Nicholas," the old man said. Slowly the lion's mane subsided, and with one more growl in Jonah's direction and a flick of his tail, he strolled back behind the couch and lay down again.

"Come closer, Jonah," Captain Aquille called. "Nicholas was king of the lions on the Mainland. Now that his son rules the pride, he has retired to my garden as a self-appointed bodyguard. He is a little overprotective, but you are safe."

Slowly, keeping an eye on the massive lion, Jonah approached and fell on his knees to hug the captain, shocked to see how frail the old man was. His skin was ashen, and the arms that responded to Jonah's embrace could barely hold him.

"I'm sorry," Jonah whispered. "It was my fault."

"No, my boy, I allowed it to happen," the old man murmured. "It had to happen. It's what I had to do, and now that it's over, my body can go to its rest."

Jonah shook his head and opened his mouth, but the old man held up his hand.

"Don't say anything," he said. "You will do what is necessary. With my help, you have risen from the sleeping place of your old world, and with Azrel's help, you are unburied in Mysterion. You are ready now to rescue your father from Geist and his Djinn."

Jonah paled. "But I don't know this…Mysterion. I can't fight the Djinn by myself!"

"You can and you will. As for Mysterion, I will tell you what you need to know. Azrel will tell you the rest as you go along, or else you will discover it for yourself."

"But Captain…"

"Call him 'Sire,'" Azrel said.

"What do you mean?" Jonah said, annoyed.

"You should address Monvieil by his title," Azrel said.

Jonah turned to the old man. "*You* are Monvieil…?" But he wasn't really asking. Somehow it made sense.

"I am both Captain Aquille *and* Monvieil."

Jonah frowned.

Monvieil smiled. "Perhaps I should start from the beginning then."

"But Cap – Sire, I don't…"

"There's no time, Jonah. If you want to rescue your father, you must listen to me and do as I say. Now why don't you sit down here." He patted the couch. "Trust me and then trust yourself."

"Is that appropriate, Sire?" Azrel asked. "After all…"

"Azrel!"

"Forgive me, Sire. I merely meant –"

"I know what you meant, and you must trust me too. Now sit down, Jonah."

"Good," Monvieil said when Jonah was seated comfortably. "Now let's begin at the beginning."

Chapter 12

HOW MYSTERION WAS LOST

"In the beginning," Monvieil said, "Mysterion was tranquil and the human race was united in peace with the dragons and mermaids, the lions, the unicorns and hummingbirds, the butterfly children, the phoenix and many others, some known now only in legends and magical tales.

"Together, human beings and other creatures talked as friends, in a language without words. They fed from trees of edible diamonds that nourished them with gentleness and wisdom and love. And in the tops of the trees and in the skies, the Angeli, the most ancient of creatures, guarded those below from the enemies of the Wind.

"Then came the Djinn, spawned in the chaos outside Mysterion. They are most content in the void, places without form, and most are harmless, preferring the company of their own tribes. Only the Shaitan Djinn sought to

81

spread chaos beyond its boundaries. In time they entered
Mysterion and sought to undo the work of the Wind."

Jonah frowned. "Wait, I don't understand. What is the
work of the Wind?"

"The Wind made Mysterion," Monvieil explained. "It
formed the land and sea and sky, and ordered them all. The
Wind fills all things and gives them life. Those who share
the Wind's breath share one mind and one heart, and are
truly at peace with one another."

"But how can it do all that? It's just, well, *wind*."

"'Wind' is a name we use, because it blows wherever it
wills. Really, it is without form and nameless. But because
we need to name things, we call it the Wind."

"So how did it make Mysterion?" Jonah asked.

Monvieil smiled. "To tell you the truth, I can't explain
it all. It just *blew*, and Mysterion formed. Then the Wind
encircled its creation to keep back chaos. It is this bound-
ary the Shaitan Djinn hope to break down and so annex
Mysterion.

"When they first invaded, they came in disguise and at
night. The Djinn love to work in disguise – as insects, ani-
mals, birds and even human beings, when the need suits
them. But in their first encounters, they disguised themselves as subtle and pleasant dreams. The dreamers found
themselves alone in Mysterion, and each was a king or
queen, commanding every creature absolutely. In these
dreams, the dreamers were endlessly happy, happier than
when they were awake because they did not have to share
their glory, and all the creatures of Mysterion worshipped
them alone.

"So it was that many in Mysterion came to prefer their
dreams to waking life. When they were not sleeping, they

were irritable and quarrelsome, resentful of their responsibilities and of the power of the Wind, the real ruler of Mysterion. The sleepers came to be called *Letheis* – which means 'forgetful ones' – because they wanted to forget the life they had been given. They allied themselves with the Djinn against the Wind and its people, and tried to take control of Mysterion, attacking in ships and on the backs of the flying Djinn, wielding swords forged in the fires of chaos."

Jonah was incredulous. "They fought over *dreams*?"

"Dreams are powerful things, Jonah. They shape the way we think about the world."

"I suppose…" Then Jonah shrugged and smiled. "Sorry to interrupt, Sire. Please go on."

"Interrupt all you like. You need to understand the way things really are. At first, the Angeli rallied the people of the Wind against the enemy. They armed them with diamond swords and fed them on waters from above the heavens so that they could resist the Djinn-inspired dreams.

"But even with the help of the Angeli, the people of the Wind never grew skilled in the ways of war. Some gave up, allowing themselves to be seduced by the Letheis. The others were cut down in battle, their corpses carried by the mermaids to be buried in the depths of the sea. At last, only one remained. A girl named Tinashe stood alone against a host of enemies. She fought them with her diamond sword and her Angelus Lamp for one hundred days, until she was near death.

"She made her last stand on a mountain in the middle of Mysterion, as the Letheis and Djinn descended out of the clouds. As they approached, she raised the lamp and chanted to the Wind: "One filling all, lift me forever to you!" And with her last breath, she blew Wind-Fire from her lamp, killing a thousand enemies before being cut into pieces so small that no mermaid could find her body to bury."

Jonah rubbed his eyes. They felt as if they were full of sand.

"You are tired," Monvieil said.

"A little. My brain is overflowing."

"Why don't you get some sleep. We will continue tomorrow. Azrel, show him to the bower." Monvieil gripped Jonah's shoulder. "It is good that you are here, finally."

Azrel led Jonah through the garden. The light had dimmed to the colour of old gold. Under the trees, the unicorns slept with their heads together, their horns crossed like swords. Scattered over the branches and among the bushes, the wings of the butterfly children closed and opened in time with their breathing.

"Will the light go out?" Jonah asked.

"No. It dims and brightens, but here it is always light."

They reached the far corner of the garden — bordered by a hedge, beyond which the mountain rose almost vertically. There a grove of almond trees and palms had been woven into a living shelter.

"This is where Monvieil sleeps," Azrel said.

"But I don't want to take his place."

"You won't. He sleeps on his couch as well, at least when he wishes to enter Lethes."

"Lethes?"

Azrel nodded. "The place where the Letheis went after they won."

"But how does Cap... How does Monvieil get there?"

Azrel held up her hand. "Sleep. Tomorrow I'll show you around the island, and tomorrow night, he'll explain the rest. You have to know everything to continue your quest."

"Quest?"

Azrel rolled her eyes. "To find your father, of course! Now go to sleep. I will be back in the morning, not too early."

"All right," he muttered. "See you in the morning."

Azrel nodded and fluttered upwards.

"Azrel!" She paused and looked down at him.

"Thanks for unburying me."

Jonah ducked into the bower. Inside was a small bed dressed with purple linens and a silver-cased pillow. Before he could wonder what made the pillow so soft, a dreamless sleep overcame him.

Chapter 13

HOW MYSTERION WAS FOUND

The next day, Azrel showed Jonah over Monvieil's island. There were no formal towns, but houses clustered around the sturdiest trees, standing on impossibly thin bamboo stilts, with walls and roofs intricately woven from palm leaves. Beneath the houses, sitting on stools or lying in hammocks, the elderly ate golden-apples one slice at a time. When Azrel introduced Jonah, they greeted him with a ragged chorus of "Welcome home," before returning to their conversations.

"Why did they say that?" Jonah asked.

"Because Mysterion is everyone's real home."

As he followed the Angelus along the worn footpaths, Jonah caught glimpses of rivers where women chatted while waiting for their clothes to dry on the rocks. Children darted among the shadows of the coconut trees, kicking up sand in their games. Past the trees and white sand was the expanse of ocean. Far beyond the line of the reef, fishermen stood in slender boats, casting their nets onto the silver surface, while above, the Angeli circled and dove, tracing patterns of spirals and flowers over the blue dome of the sky.

"Angeli's Island," Azrel said, pointing right, where another sun seemed to be rising.

"It's so bright," Jonah said, shielding his eyes.

"Only to humans. *We* can see it fine."

That evening, Jonah was the guest of honour at a banquet on the beach. Trestle tables had been set up around the edge of a well-trodden clearing among the coconut trees. As the sun set, the people lit lanterns on ropes stretched between the trunks. Nearer the beach, a group of men wrapped gutted and spiced red snappers, lobsters and crabs in banana leaves, laid them on a bed of coals, then shovelled more white-hot embers over them.

In groups of two or three, people emerged from the trees, laden with platters of desserts and salads, placing them on a table to one side before coming forward to greet Jonah with kisses on both his cheeks. When everyone was seated, young girls in flaring, pleated skirts and white blouses brought around jugs of coconut milk and palm wine. Jonah held out his glass for the wine.

"You're too young for that," Azrel said, with an amused smile. Then she held out her own glass to be filled.

"You're no older than me!"

"I am older than you can ever imagine. Besides, I'm an Angelus. The rules don't apply."

"Well, whoopee for you," Jonah muttered, allowing the girl to fill his glass with coconut milk.

When everyone's glass was filled, a middle-aged man with ebony skin and green eyes stood to offer a toast:

"To our absent Elder and his health! And to our newest brother! We welcome you in the Name of the Wind."

"*Santé*!" cried the people. "Welcome!"

Jonah felt his face grow hot.

"Say something," Azrel whispered.

Jonah hesitated, then said, "Thank you for receiving me," and sat down, amid a round of applause and clinking glasses.

"Eloquent."

"Shut up, Azrel," Jonah muttered.

Then the men uncovered the cooking pit in clouds of fragrant steam and the girls who served the wine brought around mountainous platters of fish and seafood, palm-heart salad and breadfruit fritters. Jonah's irritation at Azrel vanished. Watching the faces of Monvieil's people lit by the golden light of the lanterns, his anxiousness of the past weeks receded and contentment drifted over him. He ate his fill of the most delicious food he had ever tasted. When they brought desserts, he tasted the nougat, decided that it was almost as good as his mother's, and piled his plate full.

After the tables were cleared, men and women formed lines facing partners. Three toothless old men played mandolin, triangle and drums, while a fourth fiddled and called out instructions to the couples, who shuffled back and forth, hands on hips, circling each other in time to the music.

Jonah recognised the dance and grinned. "The *Sega*! You have the *Sega*!"

"If you say so." Azrel shrugged. "We just call it the Dance of Circles."

During the third round of the dance, Azrel tapped Jonah's shoulder and gestured at the moon, newly risen in the sky.

"We should go," she said. "Monvieil is expecting you back."

"But this is fun."

"This is still the beginning, Jonah," Azrel said softly.

"Shouldn't I say goodbye?"

"No. They cannot know why you are leaving."

Jonah considered arguing the point, but feeling his old anxiety tying knots in his stomach, he slipped away from the table and followed the Angelus into the forest. No one seemed to notice their departure, so caught up were they in the fiddler's instructions.

Azrel led him through the quiet forest and back up the hill into Monvieil's garden. The old man had aged: his hair looked like smoke and his skin had turned the colour of parchment.

After Jonah had knelt and greeted him, Monvieil asked in a hoarse voice: "So Jonah, what do you think of my island and my people?"

"No one seems afraid. And they love to dance."

"That's true. It is a very peaceful place. But even here, we have our problems."

"Like what?"

"Well, sometimes people leave because they are not happy."

"Why would they not be happy?"

"Because they are weak, and the Djinn have exploited their weakness."

"Like with the people they took before. The Leth – something."

"The Letheis." Monvieil nodded. "Yes, and the Djinn are still lurking, though there are fewer of them now and they are weaker. Before my time, the Djinn were able to put the whole of Mysterion under the spell of their illusions."

"That was after they killed that girl, right? The last one."

"Tinashe. Then they covered the face of Mysterion like locusts, eating every growing thing, until the land was barren and stinking with their droppings. In the skies, the Wind raged for its people in an endless monsoon storm, but Mysterion became a wasteland, a place of endless winter.

"The Angeli flew into exile above the heavens, while the surviving creatures huddled in their secret places underground and underwater, emerging only in utter darkness to brave the storm for a while in order to gather scraps to eat before heading for shelter again.

"The triumphant Letheis soon gave up living in this harsh reality and returned to their endless sleeping. Soon, they forgot about their bodies, which shrank to mere husks. They lived only in their dreams, which flowed out as streams into the earth of Mysterion until they gathered into an ocean at the base of the world, a single collective dream in which people had to compete to regain their old, pleasant fantasies of ruling the world. They no longer ate diamond fruits, but hoarded them as wealth. They no longer befriended the creatures of the land, but used them to gain advantage over one another, or simply forgot about them, like the dragon, the unicorn and the butterfly children. So it was that the sleeping Letheis gave birth to what you would call the ordinary world, but what we call *Lethes*, the world of those who forgot to wake up."

"So..." Jonah paused. "My world is a *dream*?"

"Yes."

"And Maman and Papa. Are they a dream too?"

"No. They are real in Mysterion, like all the Letheis."

"And they are asleep."

Monvieil nodded. "Your mother is buried somewhere, just as you and your father were."

"Don't you know where?"

"No. We only know when someone wakes up. The Angeli can hear their Mysterion hearts beating."

Jonah considered this strange idea for a moment.

"So Dad isn't buried?"

"Not any more. The Djinn unburied him when he purchased the Chant."

"But why were we buried in the first place?" This was all starting to sound a little crazy.

"The earth slowly covered all the Letheis as they slept. In time, they put forth offspring who were as asleep as they were. And as each of the Letheis died in their world, they entered a suspended state in this one, while their offspring continued the line in new shoots that grew continuously downward in Mysterion, each generation deeper than the one before it, like an immense upside down tree in the heart of this world."

"So that's how I was born then?"

"Yes, and how your parents were born. And their parents before them all the way back to the dark time, what we call the Age of the Djinn. Over those first Letheis grew forests of stunted trees that fed on the rivulets of their dreams and bore foul-tasting Black Fruit. By this time, the Djinn were starving, and made their homes in the branches of these Nightmare trees. For hundreds of years, they did little more than feed on the Black Fruit and protect themselves from the rage of the Wind.

"But the Djinn could not desecrate all of Mysterion. High up on the mountain, the place where Tinashe had died remained untouched. There a slender plant was fed by her disintegrated body. It had no branches or leaves, but at its tip swelled a single purple bud that grew larger over the centuries. At last it opened, and in its center lay an infant: Tinashe's son, born long after his mother died.

"He grew in the enclosed garden, fed water by the Angeli and fruit from the remnant of Mysterion's jewel trees. Then, in the fullness of time, he was called by the Wind to be the Elder of Mysterion. And the Elder put on his gold-and-silver tunic and his crown woven of diamonds, and he called the Wind to stop blowing and the cloud to be lifted, the rain to stop falling. As sunlight broke out, the creatures emerged from their hiding places, and stood blinking in the sunlight, but the Djinn huddled away from the light in their Nightmare trees. Then the Elder of Mysterion stood at the top of the mountain, held up an Angelus Lamp, and blew Wind-Fire over the land.

"The Djinn were consumed in an instant, along with all their filth, and their ashes flew back into chaos. The Nightmare trees, the foul weeds that grew around them – everything that bore the memory of the Djinn – burned as the Elder washed Mysterion with a cleansing fire.

"The fire entered the hearts of all his loyal creatures and burned away the years of darkness brought by the Djinn. And when all was clean, they slept with joy and peace.

"But when the Elder lay down to sleep, he willed himself to enter into the dream world of Lethes, and began to wake the Letheis, his lost people, and unbury them in Mysterion. And so he came to be known as Monvieil, because he was the first, and therefore the eldest of the human race to return to the life that had been lost."

Chapter 14
JONAH IS SENT

The garden echoed with the final words of the story. Azrel stood with her head bowed and her eyes closed, as if deep in thought or prayer. Only the black-maned lion had not stirred from his sleep behind the couch.

Jonah finally broke the silence.

"So you entered Lethes and became Captain Aquille."

"Yes," Monvieil said. "I fell asleep here and I began at my – at his – beginning, holding on to only one clue to my true identity by appearing to him in a childhood dream. When I was thrown overboard and I met the man of light, I did not realise it, but I was seeing myself as I have always been, but the discovery was not complete until I dreamed of him a second time…

"Then I took up the task of bringing the Letheis back to their true home. I tried to guide your father, but in the end, the Djinn's temptations were more seductive to him…"

"I thought you had destroyed the Djinn," Jonah interjected quickly, steering the conversation away from his father.

"I cast them into exile with Wind-Fire, but as long as there are human beings willing to be tempted, they continue to exist. They found the unburied people difficult to convert, though once in a while they had some success."

"So people leave?"

"Yes. However, only rarely. So the Djinn entered Lethes to tempt humans seeking a lost paradise – Shangri-La, the Garden of Eden, El Dorado. They promise treasure, youth, happiness, anything that you could want, all for the mere price of the Chant. And what is the price? Very simple, Jonah. What the Djinn want are their nightmares."

"That's it?" Jonah shook his head. "Nightmares?"

"The Djinn gain their strength from humanity's fears, which find their way into nightmares. During the occupation, the Letheis' dreams fed the Nightmare trees, and the trees gave fruit that the Djinn ate. When they returned to Mysterion, the Djinn brought a single Tree. They imprison in it those who owe them the price of the Chant. The enchantment in the tree brings sleep to the prisoner, but inspires endless nightmares, and the tree grows its fruit. Only the Djinn can eat the fruit without dying, for it strengthens their anger and rebellion against the Wind."

Monvieil took a deep breath and stared towards the Seeing Pools. Then he continued.

"As the Djinn gain strength from the fruit, their prisoners are drained. In time, the prisoners' nightmares consume them, and their waking moments are filled with darkness and fear and their offspring – anger, suspicion, the instinct to preserve oneself at the expense of others. Their blood becomes cold as death, almost void of human feeling. In short, they are empty and of no more use. The Djinn reward them with a chest of gold and offer a return to Lethes; but by then most Letheis have lost interest in their former lives. The Djinn send them to the islands near Nihil, to live out the rest of their lives with their fellows. I am surprised those poor souls have not killed one another for the sake of their treasure, but they have organised themselves as 'pirates,' and they call the strongest among them 'king.'"

"Will Papa turn into a pirate?"

"That was his decision," Monvieil replied. "Yes."

"No." Jonah's voice shook. "He must have been tricked. He wouldn't have given us up for that."

"That may be, but –"

"They're liars! You said so yourself!"

Monvieil looked at him a long while. "Well," he said finally, "you must discover the truth for yourself."

"I'm going to rescue my father," Jonah replied hotly. "That's all there is to it!"

"Very well," Monvieil said. "Do what you need to do. But if you are going, you must go now. There's no time to waste, now that you are here. It seems the Djinn have special plans for you. They have gone to a lot of effort to tempt you, and even offered you a special incentive."

"They offered Papa."

"A strong incentive. Your refusal did you credit."

Jonah shrugged away the compliment. "What plans do they have?"

"I am not sure, but it may have something to do with their quest to return to power in Mysterion."

"Is that why Geist didn't attack me in Lethes?" Jonah said. "Because he needs me for something?"

"Possibly. Whatever it is, you can be sure that it will involve enslavement and death. You must be very careful how you proceed."

"Do the Djinn know that I am here?" Jonah asked, looking around.

"Perhaps," Monvieil replied. "Quite possibly."

"Then how can I…" Jonah's voice trailed into silence.

"Just listen to the Wind," he said. "You will know. Other than that, you can only take the next step forward."

"So what *is* that?"

"You must go," Monvieil replied. "Now."

"How…" Jonah stuttered. "How will I get there? By boat…?"

Monvieil shook his head.

"Too slow. You must travel quickly, in the air, while you're close to the heart of Mysterion. After that, you can go by water. The mermaids can help you. Once you reach the Djinn's unmarked island, you will need to get in somehow. I'm afraid that you're on your own there, but perhaps the mermaids will have a suggestion… When it is over, the Angeli will meet you and bring you and your father back here… Azrel!"

Azrel floated forward. Monvieil made a silent request and the Angelus inclined her head.

"If you insist, Sire." She gestured at Jonah. "Well, get on."

"Do I have to?"

"Don't mind Azrel," Monvieil smiled. "I think the Wind gave her a double portion of lip."

Jonah laughed and Azrel pouted. "A few jokes! But Sire, he gave as good as he got −"

"Good," the old man interrupted. "Now Azrel, Jonah needs to keep his mind on what he is doing. You will not distract him. Do you understand?"

"Yes, Sire," Azrel said, rolling her eyes.

"And Jonah," the old man said, "Azrel likes a good back-and-forth, but she has all my confidence. Believe it or not, you can trust her – and learn from her."

"Yes, Sire."

"Good. Now before you go, I have something to give you. Azrel, could you?"

Azrel floated up into the tree and descended with an Angelus Lamp of silver inlaid with tiny diamonds. Azrel handed the lamp to Monvieil, who placed it in Jonah's hands.

Jonah was surprised at how light the lamp was.

"Although it is smaller, this is much like the one you used in Lethes," Monvieil said. "It, too, reveals things as they really are. But this one shines out Wind-Fire."

"You mean, what Tinashe used?" Jonah asked.

"Yes."

"Isn't that what happened when I blew on the other lamp?"

"No," the old man said. "You can learn to reveal Mysterion, but kindling Wind-Fire is not something you can be taught. It is a gift that only the Wind can give, and only those who first trust in the Wind can send it forth to destroy their enemies."

"So how will I know whether –?"

"You'll know," Monvieil laughed. "Or not. For now, don't worry about it. Just trust in the Wind…"

Azrel put the lamp into a bag made of thick black cloth. She showed Jonah how it could be opened by a tug on a drawstring, then helped him sling it on his back and tighten the straps.

"When you're ready to use the lamp, reach back and pull it up and out," Azrel explained. "All right?"

Jonah nodded, trying to adjust the straps so they didn't pinch so much.

"And don't loosen the straps."

"She's right, Jonah," Monvieil said. "Without the lamp, you will certainly be defeated."

"Okay, okay!" Jonah brushed away Azrel's hands and tightened the straps again.

"Good." Monvieil smiled. "Now you are ready. Come and say goodbye."

Jonah hugged the old man.

"I will be with you," Monvieil said. "Listen to the Wind."

"Yes, Sire."

"Now, off you go."

"Yes, come on, Jonah!" Azrel said. "We don't have time for tears!"

"I'm coming!" Jonah cried.

"Try not to kill each other before you get there." Monvieil waved as Azrel rose into the air. "One more thing, Jonah." Monvieil's voice was hoarse, his body pale, almost translucent.

"Yes, Sire?"

"Whatever happens, remember how Tinashe triumphed against the host of Djinn and Letheis. A love like hers is the key to your father's prison."

Jonah did not know what he meant, but for some reason the words brought tears into his eyes.

"Yes, Sire," he said. Then: "And Sire? If I don't come back, will you tell my mother what happened?"

"Don't worry. I have given her a dream to comfort her."

At that moment, King Nicholas lifted his head and let out a roar that Jonah took to mean farewell in the language of lions. He waved.

Azrel rose swiftly until the island lay spread below them, dotted with the soft lights of Angeli standing guard. She circled the island once. Jonah clung desperately to her shoulders. He was starting to get nauseous and decided that Azrel was doing this just to frighten him; but she straightened out and the island disappeared behind them.

After they left, a buzzing began in the tree above Monvieil's couch. A moment later, a bluebottle darted out from among the leaves and spun up into the darkness. King Nicholas growled, but Monvieil spoke without opening his eyes.

"Yes, I know," he murmured. "And you may think me heartless, but it must be allowed. For now."

King Nicholas grunted doubtfully and lay his head back on his paws.

"Do not worry, my friend, it will be well. In the Wind, it will *always* be well."

Jonah and Azrel flew over the brilliance of Angeli Island. "We don't have time to stop!" Azrel shouted over the wind. "But if you think it's beautiful from this distance, maybe when you get back with your dad, I'll take you on a tour!"

She believes I'm coming back, Jonah thought, and he felt a rush of affection for the sharp-tongued Angelus.

"Thanks, Azrel!" he shouted.

Azrel looked back and smiled. "You're welcome! Now, why don't you get some sleep. I have to watch for Djinn!"

Jonah nodded. Angeli Island had disappeared over the horizon and the ocean glittered and heaved in the moonlight. As beautiful as the sight was, Jonah soon felt his eyelids drooping. His arms relaxed and he started to slip from the Angelus' back. Azrel reached back and pulled him up, but Jonah was too exhausted to stir.

"Welcome home, Your Highness," she whispered.

High above, the bluebottle buzzed, doggedly following them into the West.

Chapter 15

THE ODYSSEY OF JONAH

Jonah woke to the sensation of Azrel descending below him. They were sinking towards the ocean, a gold sheet under the rising sun.

"We're here," Azrel said. "Mermaid Island."

"What island?" Jonah slurred, still groggy from sleep.

"Down there."

Jonah rubbed his eyes and forced them to focus. He could see into the clear water, all the way to the bottom, and the sight that met his eyes jolted him fully awake.

Rising from the floor of the ocean was a mound of swaying seaweed. From its centre grew a thick-limbed takamaka tree so huge that the tips of its tallest branches broke the surface.

Glittering in the sunbeams, mermaids rose in their hundreds to meet Jonah and Azrel. None of them resembled the pictures of mermaids that Jonah had seen, and he held his breath in amazement. Their upper bodies formed every colour and shape. They had pleated their hair into unlikely sculptures on their heads, while their lower bodies were finned like angelfish, bass, dolphins, sharks and even the tentacles of an octopus. All wore gold necklaces laced with precious gems, woven silver bangles, and most were also armed with scimitars and javelins, so that Jonah wondered how they even managed to keep from sinking, let alone swim.

"There's Queen Zoë." Azrel pointed.

"Which one?" They all looked like royalty to Jonah.

"The one in front," Azrel replied. "Blue skin. Silver tiara."

Jonah saw her then – a slender mermaid with a gentle, heart-shaped face and the tail of a seahorse. Something about her reminded him of his mother, and a wave of sadness broke over him. The mermaids surfaced in an uproar of foam and crowded in to greet them. They reminded Jonah of the women who came to the beach at dawn to wait for the fishing boats and exchange gossip, and when the boats sped out of the sunrise and up onto the sand, the women jostled each other and shouted bids to the grinning fishermen for the best of the catch.

Now the crowd moved aside and Queen Zoë swam forward to greet them.

"You are welcome to our realm, young Jonah," she said. Her voice sounded like a stream flowing over pebbles.

"Thank you, but how do you know my name?"

"We saw and heard you through our Seeing Pool."

"Could everyone know about me from those pools?" It was an unnerving thought.

"No, no. Only those to whom Monvieil wishes to reveal his mind. But he spoke to us of you, and we are ready to serve both you and the honourable Azrel."

Azrel inclined her head. "We certainly could use your help, Your Majesty."

"And you shall have it. But first things first. Some breakfast for Jonah, I think."

"Um," Azrel began. "We are in somewhat of a hurry −"

"Nonsense. The young man has not eaten since last night."

She clapped her hands, and a moment later, a large, polished clamshell broke the surface, carried on the shoulders of two mermaids. Another brought a low table set with a mother-of-pearl bowl and a silver goblet, and rested it in the shell.

"Please have a seat, Jonah."

Relieved to get off his perch, Jonah slid from Azrel's back, onto the floating shell. He settled himself cross-legged, adjusting his knapsack to make the bulk of the lamp a little more comfortable.

Queen Zoë turned to Azrel. "Please forgive me, Guardian, for we are unable to offer you acceptable hospitality."

"You will just have to grow wings, I'm afraid," Azrel said with a smile.

The mermaid queen's laugh sounded like waves. "We will do that when you learn how to swim." Then she turned to Jonah. "Please begin, Master Jonah. We have already eaten."

Jonah's insides turned over; the cup contained an opaque white liquid and the bowl held a soup of some kind, with pieces of octopus tentacles and prawns and strips of what must be seaweed. It reminded Jonah of a *bouillon* his mother had once made, one of the few meals that he did not like. Still, she had made him eat – it had taken him an hour. The eyes of the mermaids were on him, as if waiting for his praise. Azrel, too, was looking at him, her face studiously expressionless. *She's waiting to see if I'll chicken out,* he thought.

At that thought, he picked up the silver spoon and began to shovel in the soup. It was cold and salty, and the seafood was raw. Jonah steeled himself and chewed for what seemed like an eternity. Just as he was about to retch, he grabbed the cup and took a large swallow, closing his eyes in anticipation of whale milk or something equally foul tasting. To his delight, it was coconut milk. He took several swallows, washing the taste of fish from his mouth.

"Very good," he said. "Thank you."

"You don't want more?" the queen asked, her eyes wide.

Jonah shook his head as calmly as he could manage. "No, no. That was just perfect."

"A growing boy like you?" Azrel chuckled. "Have some more!"

"I'm stuffed," Jonah said, giving her a threatening look.

"Well…" Queen Zoë shrugged, "…if you are certain."

"Yes, thank you," Jonah replied, his stomach aching with hunger.

"Then we will begin immediately, I think," the queen said. "It is a long journey. And if you do not mind me asking," she looked at Jonah, "how do you intend to get into the Djinn island when we get there?"

Azrel frowned down at the queen.

"We were hoping Your Majesty could tell us that," she said. "Monvieil indicated that you might –"

"The unmarked island is well guarded by Djinn magic. The only humans to enter and leave are pirates. We can guide you there, but as for getting in…"

"But I thought he said you knew." Disappointment drenched Jonah's heart.

Queen Zoë shook her head. "He said only that we *might* know of a way. He is the Son of the Wind. He knows the depths of our hearts, but not the movement of every ripple in Mysterion. I am truly sorry," she said. "The only ones who know are the pirates."

Something buzzed in Jonah's ear and he swiped it away.

"What is it?" Azrel asked sharply. "Why did you do that?"

"A fly," Jonah replied, watching the black speck spin upwards into the clear sky.

"Not this far out on the ocean." Azrel looked at Queen Zoë, who nodded.

"Then they probably know." Azrel said.

Jonah frowned. "Who know?"

"That fly was probably a Djinn spy. Chances are they know of your plan by now."

"So what do we do?"

Azrel shrugged. "We keep going and trust the Wind."

"That's all?"

"What else?"

"I mean, shouldn't we have a plan?"

"Monvieil sent us to the mermaids," Azrel said quietly. "Perhaps a way will make itself known. But it's your quest. You decide."

Jonah looked at Queen Zoë, who smiled in a quiet way that reminded him so suddenly and forcefully of his mother that tears came into his eyes.

"Please lead us, Your Highness," he said and climbed on Azrel's back.

The mermaids formed up on either side of their queen and they set off, leading the way. They spent the next day travelling over the ocean realm of the mermaids. As they went, Queen Zoë pointed out the sights on the seabed. Jonah saw the Plain of Wrecks, where the mermaids had gathered the sunken ships of the Letheis and the pirates from the corners of Mysterion. Jonah saw Arabian dhows, European square-riggers, flying Dutchmen, schooners and strange, cylindrical-shaped ships with round sails that he did not recognise. All were intact, with sails set, as if ready to surface and continue their plunder.

"We preserve them," Zoë said. "Their evil must not be forgotten, even in the Higher Mysterion."

"Higher Mysterion?"

"The coming time. When the suspended Letheis are raised…"

"You mean the dead?" Jonah exclaimed. "The dead in my world?"

"I suppose so. The sleeping Letheis will be awakened by Monvieil and decide whether to live in the Wind. Those who refuse will follow the Djinn into exile. Those who say yes will be restored in joy to Mysterion."

"Like it was at the beginning," said Jonah, remembering Monvieil's story.

Zoë shook her head and smiled. "Better than the beginning."

They travelled above the Swaying Mountains, tall pillars of soft red coral, through which an army of mermaids swept, driving fish beyond the Mountains to a plain of white sand and seaweed clusters.

"We graze the shoals there before moving them closer to Monvieil's island," Zoë said. "Then we herd them into the fishermen's nets to feed the people of the Wind."

Past the plains, a pair of dragons frolicked. They reminded Jonah of golden retrievers with the bodies of serpents. Their stumpy wings propelled them a few feet above the surface before they slapped down, drenching the convoy with spray. In the end, Queen Zoë grew tired of their antics and shooed them away to play a hunting game with a shoal of red snapper.

With the sun setting in their faces, they paused to eat a dinner of sea cucumber, crab salad and more coconut milk. His hunger even more intense now, Jonah found that he could swallow the raw meat without gagging, and his thanks to Queen Zoë was genuine.

She smiled in return. "You are a worthy boy. Most humans never learn to stomach our food. You almost threw up only once!"

Realizing then that she had seen through his little ruse that morning, Jonah blushed.

The queen laughed. "Your politeness was charming — and unusual in one your age."

When night came over the sea, the mermaids carved brilliant paths of phosphorescence through the waters for Azrel to follow. When the moon rose, huge and silver above the horizon, Jonah thought about home — the dinner his mother and Madame Paul would have cooked (oh, for a pork curry with mango salad!); the scent of lilacs in her perfume; and his own bed. As sleep overtook him he wondered if she had stopped looking for him yet, or if she sat every day at the high-tide mark, watching for his sail to rise above the horizon...

I'm sorry, Maman, he thought. *If you can hear me, I'm really sorry.*

How would this end, he wondered. Were the things Monvieil told him about his father really true? He had put on a defiant face, but if they were true, if his father had… But then why had Monvieil sent Jonah to find him? *Love will open any prison*, the old man had said, but that was just vague nothingness, not a solution. And even if Jonah could free him, would his father want to leave? Hadn't he found the treasure he had been looking for?

These questions were too much and he abandoned them. He leaned forward.

"I can't sleep," he said to Azrel.

"You shouldn't have to," she replied. "Sleep is a waste of time."

"You don't sleep?"

"Huh!" Azrel sniffed. "Angeli, sleep? Never! We are guardians, always wakeful."

"I like sleeping, especially on weekends."

"How do you know? You're asleep!"

Jonah thought about this for a moment.

"Okay, maybe not the sleeping part," he admitted. "But I like waking up late and I like going to sleep when I know I don't have to get up for school the next morning."

"You mean you like not worrying about time – deadlines and schedules."

"I suppose. But it's nice just to be quiet sometimes."

"So it's peace you like."

"Perhaps, yes." Jonah nodded. "Just not worrying what's going to happen."

"That was the way all human beings lived before the time of the Letheis."

"Really?"

"Yes. And if the Wind blows that way, it will be so again."

"In the Higher Mysterion?"

Azrel smiled. "You learn pretty quick – *for a boy*."

"Mouthy and sarcastic – just like a girl!"

Azrel laughed and did a quick somersault, making Jonah gasp and clutch at her.

As the night turned blue, their conversation faded into companionable silence. As dawn spread over the ocean, Azrel pointed ahead and Jonah saw a small island. It rose abruptly out of the sea, perfectly rounded, slick with algae and crusted with barnacles, as if the island had been submerged.

As they came closer, Jonah realized the island was made up of many rocks, each regularly shaped, six-sided and fitting perfectly together, like a mosaic, the whole island descending steeply to the sandbar on which it was resting, as if a giant hand had simply dropped it there.

"It looks like –" Jonah started.

"Wait," Azrel said. "Watch."

As the mermaids angled away to pass the sandbar, the island rose and slid forward, propelled by a pair of giant flippers. A rounded head with narrow eyes emerged, stretching almost half the length of its body. The flippers pulled the whole bulk forward, and the giant tortoise dove beneath the surface in an explosion of water.

"Qahal," Azrel explained. "He's shy."

Jonah just shook his head in awe.

"Just wait," Azrel warned. "There's more to come."

Chapter 16

THE CYCLOPS AND THE PIRATE

Beyond Qahal's sandbar, Mysterion seemed to run out of sights. The emptiness of ocean and sky merged into a single blue.

Then an island rose up on the horizon, a heap of granite boulders and smaller rocks, but apart from a coconut tree at its centre, totally barren. Several boats of different sizes lay on the shore, but Jonah could see no sign of their owners.

There was something familiar about the place, and Jonah searched his mind for the memory. Below, the mermaids were changing course to give the island a wide berth. As Azrel followed them, she murmured, "The Cyclops' island. We must be careful. He does not take kindly to intruders."

Jonah remembered seeing the island in Monvieil's pools. "Where is he?"

"Shh. Not so loud. He might —"

But before Azrel could finish, the water in front of them erupted, and the Cyclops rose up, dripping. He was as tall as a house, with a square face and an empty eye socket above his nose. His body was covered with hair, he wore only a blackened loincloth and he smelled of old sweat and rotting meat.

"Thank the Wind!" the giant roared. "Just when I was starting to get the rumbles, a snack arrives!"

"Mighty Cyclops!" Azrel shouted. "We come at the bidding of Monvieil."

"This is a mission of the Wind!" Queen Zoë cried below.

The mermaids had formed up around the Cyclops, their scimitars raised and javelins at the ready, but the Cyclops did not seem to notice.

"An Angelus and a host of mermaids! An unlikely combination. And what's that?" He sniffed. "The Angelus carrying a boy on its back! Now I know miracles can happen!"

"I was commanded to bring him to the unmarked island," Azrel said. "He is in search of his father."

"Ha!" the Cyclops shouted. Jonah caught a blast of the Cyclops' breath full in the face. He coughed and retched at the stench, barely containing his urge to vomit.

"A touching story," the Cyclops continued. "But I have a story too. Once there was a little pirate who decided he was going to be a nuisance to the people of the Wind. So he got together with some Djinn friends, and they pretended to be mermaids and Angeli. They pretended that he had defected and was returning his loyalty to Monvieil, but —"

"You are wrong!" Azrel said desperately.

"Let me finish!" The Cyclops snapped. "When this nasty little pirate had wreaked his havoc, he came back home, hoping that the pirate king would grant him honour and riches. But, alas, it was not to be, for along the way, he met a Cyclops who made sure that none of them would disturb the peace of Mysterion ever again!"

And even before he finished speaking, the Cyclops had crouched and was leaping up towards Azrel and Jonah in an explosion of white water. Below, the mermaids hurled their javelins, but their missiles lost their target in the confusion of the waves. Azrel, taken off guard, darted upwards so quickly that Jonah was crushed against her back, as the huge hand whistled just beneath them. Then the Cyclops crashed back into the ocean, roaring, kicking and swiping around him as the mermaids' javelins stung him.

From far above, Bagat the Djinn, still disguised as a bluebottle, flew down into Jonah's face and exploded into the form of a bat, shrieking and flapping. The boy yelled and let go of Azrel's shoulder to fend off Bagat, and as he did so, the Djinn returned to his natural form for an instant, and pushed Jonah off Azrel's back. Azrel spun around, swiping at the Djinn and grabbing for Jonah at the same time, but Jonah was already out of reach, his arms flailing.

He hit the water with a stunning, painful slap. Then he was under, and something grabbed and tried to hold him. But Jonah slid through, rising to the surface, kicking and scrabbling. Then something closed around his body and he was lifted into the air. As he painfully coughed his lungs free of water, he saw the Cyclops' shaggy head and empty eye socket staring.

Azrel darted around him, her body glittering in the sunlight. She was slashing at the Cyclops with a sword that reflected sunlight in all directions like a crystal. Below, he could hear the mermaids' warlike cries as they attacked the giant's legs. The Cyclops paid little attention, swatting at Azrel occasionally as at an annoying mosquito, and kicking up waves that repelled the mermaids.

"A bit of a shrimp, aren't you?" The Cyclops shook Jonah so his head flopped back and forth. "Well, boy, think about your fate — until it is time for dessert!"

Above, Bagat, now a fly again, panicked. *If I have to tell the Elder that the boy was eaten by the monster —!*

Realizing that Jonah was unconscious, the Cyclops stopped shaking and examined his prize. "Pirate baubles," he muttered, pulling the pack containing the Angelus Lamp off the boy and dropping it into the water. Ignoring the blows of Azrel's light sword as she circled and dived around him, screaming her frustration, the Cyclops waded to his island. When he reached the shore, he wiped the thicket of javelins off his skin and scrambled up among the rocks until he reached a huge boulder. Rolling it away, he revealed the black mouth of a cave and tossed the boy inside.

He needs a pirate, Bagat thought. *So he'll have one!* And he darted down, slipping into the cave just before the Cyclops shifted the boulder back into place.

Jonah came to, aware of the stench of the Cyclops that filled the stifling, humid air around him. Then a hand was shaking his shoulder.

"Wake up, my friend." It was the voice of a young man of about Jonah's age. Jonah tried to see his face, but the darkness was impenetrable.

"Where am I?"

"The man-eater's lair. If the smell didn't tell you already."

"And who are you?"

"I am...I was...one of Hodoul's wards," the boy said.

"Hodoul the pirate?"

"The Pirate King. No one forgets his name once he has paid them a visit. And even those who have never seen his face hear his name and their sleep is troubled thereafter."

"So you're a pirate."

"I was. But I left."

"Oh. Why?"

"I was tired."

"Tired of what?" Jonah heard the boy shift away and wondered if he had offended him.

"Reach out."

Jonah stretched out his hand until he made contact. The boy's skin was strangely cool, stretching and rippling under his hand. Then he felt ridges under his fingertips, like seams in cloth. Some of them were still damp.

"I was tired of getting those," the boy said.

Jonah could not imagine it.

"I decided Monvieil could not be any worse," the boy continued. "In spite of what they said."

"So how did you end up here?"

"This is as far as I got." The boy chuckled. "Not much of an escape. I fooled old Hodoul into thinking I was still loyal, but I couldn't convince this monster that I was actually a traitor."

"He didn't believe me either."

"Oh? And where do you come from?"

Jonah hesitated. Could he trust this boy?

"It's all right," the boy said. "You don't have to tell."

"I'm Jonah." He reached out his hand.

"Sartish," the boy said. They bumped hands and then shook. Sartish's hand was rough and his grip was fierce. Jonah wondered what crimes it had committed, but pushed the thought away. Whatever Sartish had been or still was, they were now allies.

"Pleased to meet you, Sartish. So, do you think we could find a way out of here?"

"I have been here for two days. I know every bloody rock by heart."

"So what do we do?" Jonah said, trying not to sound shocked by Sartish's language.

"I don't know…" Sartish sounded thoughtful. "But with two of us, we might be able to dream up something to fool the Cyclops. He is blind, of course, but his sense of smell is deadly. That's what always did us in on the raids…"

"Raids?"

"Yeah, whenever we went to raid the people of the Wind, he always met us. The first line of defence, we called him. It was pretty hard to get past him. Even with the wind in our faces, he sniffed us out every time. We always lost at least one ship. It got so that Hodoul assigned a ship to be a red herring…"

They were silent.

"If his sense of smell is that good, what chance do we have in this small a space?"

"I don't know…"

Then a flicker of a thought came to Jonah. "Can he tell the difference between us? By smell, I mean?"

"I don't think so. He can tell between humans and other creatures, but —"

"Can you make your voice like mine?"

"How do you mean?"

"Can you make it sound like mine?"

"I think so." Sartish paused. "How's this?" His voice sounded higher.

"Like this," Jonah said.

"Like this," Sartish repeated, a little lower.

"Better. If we practice a little before he comes, it should work."

"*What* should work?"

"My father told me a story once, about Sungula…"

"Who's Sungula?"

"He's a rabbit. A real trickster…"

Sartish snickered. "A *bunny* is going to help us?"

"I know," Jonah said quickly, feeling his face grow hot. "But just listen. Monsieur Renard the fox vowed to catch and eat the pesky Sungula once and for all. He chased and chased and chased him, until finally he chased that Sungula into a hole and put a stone over the mouth to stop him from escaping. 'You will have to come out in the end,' said Monsieur Renard. 'Come out now and I will give you a quick death!'

"But Sungula had a plan. He had learned to throw his voice to other places, which had served him well when he was stealing vegetables from Monsieur Antoine's garden. So he said to Monsieur Renard: 'One cannot eat at this time of day. I will come out at dinnertime. Then I will die quickly and you can enjoy your meal properly.'

"The fox, thinking that this sounded very civilized, agreed. He went away and returned at six o'clock, when the sun was setting. He moved the stone from the mouth of the hole and peered in, but because it was getting dark, he couldn't see much. 'Come out, little Sungula!' he cried.

'Come out for dinner!' Sungula threw his voice behind Monsieur Renard and called: 'I am out already, Monsieur! I freed myself!' Monsieur Renard turned around to see where Sungula was and the tricky rabbit ran out of the hole and escaped in the darkness. And Monsieur Renard went hungry."

Sartish was silent for a few moments.

"I see," he said, and then he gripped Jonah's shoulder. "It's brilliant. And it *does* need two voices!"

"The Cyclops will go for one of us pretty quickly," Jonah said. "But if we can confuse him, even for a few seconds... And once we're out, we'll need a quick escape."

"Easy," Sartish said. "We take a boat."

"Too slow. He'd catch as in an instant."

"Don't worry about that. My boat's the fastest in Mysterion. Besides, can you think of a faster way?"

Jonah thought.

"No," he said finally. "With the mermaids gone, I suppose a boat is it."

"You came with mermaids?"

"Yes," Jonah said. He held back saying more. He still wasn't sure about Sartish. The boy seemed almost too co-operative for a pirate, too eager to please.

"Very well," Sartish said after an awkward pause. "Let's practice your plan."

They rehearsed until the sound of shifting rock interrupted them.

"He's coming!" Sartish said.

"Positions!" Jonah hissed. They moved to opposite ends of the cave, facing each other. A moment later, the boulder rolled away from the opening, to be replaced by the square, blank face of the Cyclops.

"Dessert time!" the Cyclops shouted. "Where are you, my little dessert?"

A strange thought occurred to Jonah – *Does he realize Sartish is here?* He frowned and began to correct himself – *Of course he must* – but before he could continue, the Cyclops ducked into the cave.

"Where are you?" The Cyclops swung his head from left to right.

"Here I am," Jonah said. The Cyclops turned towards him.

"Here I am," Sartish echoed, and even Jonah was surprised at how similar his voice sounded. Confused, the Cyclops turned his head away from Jonah. "What kind of pirate trickery is this?"

Jonah moved along the wall, deeper into the cave. He knew Sartish was at the same moment moving opposite him towards the cave's entrance.

"I'm waiting, Cyclops!" Jonah said.

Again the Cyclops swung towards him. "Whatever magic you've devised, little dessert, it won't save you!"

"It just did!" Sartish shouted from the entrance.

"Damned pirates!" the Cyclops roared and dove forward as Sartish darted out of the cave.

"Are you sure you want that one?" Jonah asked.

The Cyclops paused.

"Of course he does!" Sartish said from outside.

The Cyclops stood in the entrance, hesitant. "You think you fooled me, boy. But we'll see who is who…" And he began to roll the boulder over the entrance.

Jonah panicked. He ran at the entrance, but knew he would be too late to get through.

Sartish darted up behind the Cyclops and sank his teeth into the monster's leg. The monster roared and swatted at him. Sartish ducked away, but the boulder stopped rolling long enough for Jonah to slip through the entrance. As agreed, the boys ran in opposite directions. "Here we go!" they shouted in unison.

The Cyclops roared in frustration, unable to decide which scent to follow, and so he just stood, turning left and right, his face contorted.

As he approached the water, Jonah circled along the shoreline. At the other side of the island, Sartish did the same. Jonah ducked and darted among the abandoned boats until he reached a wooden dinghy that reminded him painfully of *Albatross*. Sartish was setting the sail, and Jonah got his first good look at him – a dark-skinned boy with oil-black hair and eyes like granite pebbles.

"Hurry!" Sartish gestured. "He'll know we're together."

He was right. The Cyclops' head was turning in their direction, finding their scent.

"Help me drag her into the water," Sartish said, a little impatient.

Jonah grabbed the gunwale and together they pulled the dinghy towards the breaking surf. Jonah could hear the thump of the Cyclops' feet as he descended towards them. Rocks began to fall around them.

"Faster," Sartish panted. Jonah tried, but only succeeded in stubbing his toe. Then the dinghy's bow was into the waves, and a moment later, floating free.

"Climb in," Sartish said. Relieved, Jonah tumbled into the cockpit. His relief was momentary, however, for just as Sartish guided the dinghy out of the wind's eye –

"Now I've got you!"

The Cyclops was squatting on a boulder several feet above the beach, facing them. Sartish leapt into the boat, grabbed the tiller and pulled the mainsheet in. At once, the sails filled, and the dinghy leapt forward, heeling in the stiff wind. Jonah scrambled to windward and both boys leaned out to level the dinghy.

The Cyclops was wading after them, making surprising speed as the water exploded against his legs. As they left the shallows and entered open ocean, he broke into a clumsy dog-paddle that seemed to bring him closer with each stroke.

"He's catching up!" Jonah shouted. "We've got to go faster!"

Sartish glanced back at the Cyclops, now less than six metres away, his mat of hair slicked down over his enraged face. "We should be skimming by now. There's too much weight!"

"What do we do?" Jonah's chest felt tight with fear.

"I'll bail."

"What do you mean?"

"I'll jump off – to lighten the weight."

"No!"

"Yes. Jonah, listen to me. You were right not to trust me." His voice was barely audible over the wind.

"I was wrong," Jonah started.

"Has it occurred to you that your plan only worked because the monster believed there was only *one* person in that cave? I am not who I seem, but I do want to help you rescue your father…"

The arm of the Cyclops had hit the water less than three metres away.

"How do you know about –?"

"You will find out soon enough." Sartish reached into his filthy vest and pulled out a vial of dark liquid. "This is blood," he said. "Mine. Two drops will gain you access through the reef of fire and passage through the bay of storms."

Jonah reached out and took the vial.

"Good." Sartish nodded. "One night due west is Hodoul's island. Pass it as quickly as you can in the early morning, while everyone's still asleep. One day due west of that is Nihil. Follow the sun. Wait," he said as Jonah opened his mouth to speak. "My motives are not what they seem, but by all the Djinn, may your success be ours as well."

Sartish rolled backwards and dropped into the ocean. Unburdened, the dinghy heeled heavily, and Jonah barely had the presence of mind to grab the tiller and the main-sheet, lean out and stop her from capsizing. The dinghy's hull came level, and she darted forward just as the Cyclops' hand brushed the stern. Then the dinghy was skimming over the waves and the Cyclops' roars faded into the wind.

Jonah sailed for almost an hour towards the descending sun as he tried to sort out his thoughts. He was both thirsty and hungry, for he had eaten nothing since the previous evening. He searched the dinghy, but found nothing. He realized with mild surprise that in spite of everything, he was looking forward to what awaited him on Nihil. He had to do what Monvieil had called him to do. Whether he succeeded or failed was beside the point. Only the doing of it mattered.

Jonah leaned back – and realized that something was missing...

"The lamp!"

He looked around, as if hoping that the lamp was float-ing close by. Monvieil had told him that if he lost the lamp, the Djinn would defeat him. Now it was certain. His father was lost forever.

He took a deep breath and gripped the mainsheet.

Nothing to do now but go on, he thought grimly. *What-ever comes.*

As he pulled in the mainsail and set his course towards the sunset, he dredged his memory for the navigation les-sons his father had made him sit through and hoped to keep a westerly heading by the stars and reach Hodoul's island by dawn.

Chapter 17

THE GREATEST IMITATOR

"**S**o you went into the monster's cave with him?" the Elder Djinn asked.

"Yes, my lord," Bagat mumbled with his face in the sand. "I pretended to be imprisoned with the boy."

"What was your disguise?"

"I took the form of Sartish, Lord."

"Sartish! The boy pirate who eluded us and tricked the Cyclops last year?"

"The very one, Lord."

"He was a clever one," the Elder mused. "A real loss. Good choice… And you saw him clear of the monster?"

"I did, my lord," Bagat said. "If he sails without stopping, he should reach here by next sundown."

"And you are sure it was Jonah – dark skin, innocent face…"

"Yes."

"Not some other traitorous pirate boy the monster had caught."

"No."

The Elder was silent for a moment. Finally, he smiled. "You have done well, Bagat. Go and rest."

Bagat breathed a sigh of relief and shuffled backwards. He found a roost in one of the outlying trees and pretended to sleep, but he was really watching the Elder Djinn pace around the clearing. At last the Elder wandered off behind the Nightmare tree, and Bagat hopped surreptitiously to where Malach was pretending to doze on an upper branch.

"So you imitated Sartish?" Malach asked incredulously. "I don't believe it!"

"I've been saying it for years," Bagat boasted. "I am the greatest imitator among all the tribes of Djinn. My grandfather taught me all the subtleties of human speech and emotion. I am peerless."

"If you managed to imitate Sartish, you are, indeed. Good work, my brother."

"Thank you, my brother. Perhaps your thanks can be reflected in the honours of the new order..."

"Of course," Malach smiled. "You shall be second only to me."

"Honours indeed," Bagat said. *We will see about second*, he thought. "And now what?"

"And now we wait and see if the tyrant's prophecy is correct. If the boy defeats the Elder, we must be ready to act and gain control of the cloak and the pendant. Without them..."

The two continued to talk in whispers. They did not see the Elder Djinn under their tree, disguised as a shadow and smiling at their words.

Chapter 18

THE REEF OF FIRE
AND THE BAY OF STORMS

After a night of sailing, dizzy from exhaustion, thirst and hunger, Jonah passed Hodoul's island. The island was a forbidding-looking place, its mountains covered in impenetrable jungles and capped with cloud. Closer in to shore were anchored nine ships that looked like the ones he had seen in Monvieil's pools – dhows and square-riggers, small fishing boats, and even a dugout canoe with a mast. There were no signs of life on board. Jonah could hear nothing but the slap of water on their hulls and the tap of rigging.

He squinted at the thin line of sand along the shore. After a moment, he was able to discern the outlines of lean-tos and huts from which tendrils of smoke rose into the still dawn air. Jonah thought he could see shapes scattered across the beaches, but he could not be sure if they were human shapes, dinghies or logs.

He sailed on as quickly as he could. As the sun rose, the sea grew heavier, the waves breaking in stiff ranks against the bow. The water grew opaque, the green of a long-forgotten swamp. The splashes that fell on Jonah's skin itched and then burned as they dried.

He noticed that the light around him had grown dim and yellow. The sky was no longer blue, but a mass of brown haze sweltering under the dull, orange ball of the sun. He also became aware of the smell – a hint of sulphurous smoke that intensified until the air caught in his throat and made him cough. Fingers of smoke curled towards him, thickening into a solid bank that surrounded the boat. The wind slowed to a breeze, faltered, and failed. The sail sagged on its spar. The boat wallowed in the waves.

Then Jonah heard it – a crackling roar coming from directly ahead. His light-headedness dissolved, leaving his whole body tight with fear; but he set his face towards what he knew was the sound of Nihil. Narrowing his eyes against the smoke, tearing his throat with coughs, he pumped the tiller back and forth to propel the dinghy forward.

As he drifted, the sound grew louder, interspersed with explosions and hisses, and the tiller seemed to grow heavier and more resistant in his clutching hand.

Suddenly, through the smoke, a wall of fire rose up. Green and yellow flames curled and licked the ocean's surface, where the waves broke in a furious hissing. Clouds of steam boiled up, mingling with the smoke to block out the light above.

Jonah pushed the tiller away so that the dinghy swung parallel to the reef of fire. He pulled out the vial of Sartish's blood. *Two drops will gain you access through the reef of fire…*

What on earth had Sartish meant? How could drops of blood get him through *that*?

He tried to scull the dinghy closer to the reef of fire; but the smoke overwhelmed him, clawing at his throat and lungs. The skin on his face tightened in the heat and a moment later he smelled his hair singeing. Blind from smoke and his lungs exploding, Jonah sculled away to where he could take a few breaths again. He held up the vial and carefully removed the cork. As he did so, the boat rocked, and a drop of blood spilled onto his fingers. Instantly, Jonah felt as if his whole body had been encased in ice. The cold seized him, freezing his heart, and his mind became clear and void of emotion.

Carefully, he replaced the cork and tucked the vial back in his pocket. He knew now what Sartish had meant. One drop of blood had been enough. He turned the dinghy back towards the reef and took in the smoke like one of the fishermen who rolled their own cigarettes and lit them from the previous butt hanging from their cracked lips. As he entered the reef, the flames breathed over him, but instead of burning, he felt what seemed to be the first breeze of the morning. Only when the sail exploded into flames and the dinghy's timbers started to blacken did he realize the power of the pirate's blood.

The dinghy passed through the reef of fire, its hull smoking, but at once Jonah was confronted by a scene that overwhelmed him with terror. A monsoon storm hurled water at him in horizontal shafts that stung his arms and face, and forced him to squint. Beneath him the boat was no longer burning, for her timbers had been doused by the waves, but she was completely out of control, at the mercy of the wind's fury. Every time Jonah grabbed the tiller to get her back on course, it jerked out of his hands.

Finally, he gave up, trying to focus his thoughts. *"Two drops…"* Sartish had said.

Jonah took out the vial and tried a drop on his skin. Nothing happened. *The blood made me cold,* he thought. *And the cold countered the fire. But this is water. What would make water —*

Then the solution came to him. He balanced himself as best he could in the tossing dinghy, leaned over, and poured a drop of the pirate's blood into the water.

At once, the waves died. Only the wind continued to blow, but where it had whipped up whitecaps and green mountains of water, it now swept among frozen crests, blowing trails and spirals of ice that had been foam and water vapour. The dinghy was now still, frozen solid in the sheet of ice that had been the bay of storms.

He swung his leg over the side of the dinghy, testing the ice to see if it would hold his weight. It was solid as granite. He hopped out and carefully stepped across the ice, hugging himself against the wind that cut through his thin, torn T-shirt. At first, he guessed his direction. Then, between the frozen waves, he was able to make out an island curled on itself like a sleeping lizard.

His limbs stiffening, as if in anticipation of death, Jonah shuffled towards Nihil.

As the Wind would have it, Jonah's arrival had gone unnoticed on the beaches of Nihil. The sentry posts on the beaches were deserted, for all the Djinn had been called to the centre of the island. The clearing was packed to overflowing with murmuring Djinn, their skeletal forms glowing in the perpetual dusk. Occasional explosions of hissing broke out as one tried to force its way closer to the Nightmare tree which squatted in their midst.

Geist, the Elder Djinn, stood in front of the tree, staring expressionlessly at the host. Only one very familiar with his moods and standing very close, as both Malach and Bagat were, could perceive his satisfaction, and they now exchanged quick glances of congratulation.

The Elder Djinn raised his claw and the murmuring of the host was silenced.

"My children!" he began. "Our time is coming again!"

The Djinn hissed like wind through fallen leaves.

"Yes. The tyrant cast us out of our rightful conquest. He robbed us of the land of our inheritance…" The Djinn hissed louder, but the Elder raised his voice. "Our bodies he burned with fire and he sent us into exile. Yet we were strong, we endured and we have returned to regain what was stolen from us!"

At these words, the Djinn emitted a collective howl, which the Elder allowed for a moment before raising his claw once again. Immediately, the host was silent. They loved the Elder's speeches.

"We have harvested the tyrant's slaves and have fed on them for many years. Our restoration has come slowly – too slowly, my children – but tonight, our waiting comes to an end. If your Elder has seen rightly, tonight we shall harvest one whose sleep will restore us to full strength!"

Malach and Bagat glanced at one another. What was the Elder up to? Then he looked at them and they understood his satisfaction. *By the power of Iblis*, Malach thought.

He knows... Somehow, he knows! Bagat looked as if he wanted to sink into the earth.

"And who is this slave, you may ask?" the Elder shrieked, turning his attention back to the host. "One who has come here of his own will in order to rescue his father, our present slave. In this noble endeavour −" the Elder sneered, "− he has received assistance from unexpected sources..." He glanced down at Malach and Bagat, "...whose generosity will soon be revealed. But more than that, my children, this one has the blessing of the tyrant, who hopes the boy may be his heir!"

The Djinn fluttered and shuffled restlessly, uncertain as to what this all meant.

"To put it simply for my children," Geist went on, "this one has a special intensity of will. His sleep will be powerful and life-giving for the Tree, and the fruit borne from it will complete our powers. By his dreams the heir to the tyrant will give us his inheritance!"

The Djinn roared their approval for several minutes, while Geist looked on. *He can never have enough praise*, Malach thought with bitter envy.

At last, the Elder called for silence.

"Even now the boy is crossing the bay," he said, "and soon we will act to make the offering. Once we are whole, we shall first reward those who worked so diligently and so secretively to ensure that this boy completes his mission of mercy." The Elder seemed to smile at Malach and Bagat. Bagat shrunk away into the crowd, but Malach met the Elder's stare without flinching. "After that, we will begin our sacred mission. We shall fly towards the East and take back the land that is rightly ours!"

The Djinn roared again, and this time the Elder did not stop them. As he began a low chant, his form flickered, faded into the half-light, then reappeared as a very tall man with a bald head and eyes like holes.

Chapter 19

FRANCIS COMFAIT WALKS AWAY

J onah arrived on the shores of Nihil, his arms and legs blue from cold. As soon as he stepped onto the beach, however, he felt as if he had walked into a wall of heat. His steps slowed, sweat covered his body and ran in rivulets down his forehead. A smell like a sewer rose up at him. He retched, then held his breath and concentrated until he was under control. Then he looked around. The half-darkness he had encountered at the reef of fire persisted. The sun was no more than a brighter dullness in the cloud of steam and smoke that rose from the reef to cloak the island. The light that did filter down was blurred somehow, obscuring rather than clarifying what it touched, so that Jonah could barely discern the outlines of trees and rocks at the head of the beach.

Jonah remembered that Monvieil had said the Djinn hated light and loved working in disguise. *This is the perfect land for liars.*

Like a sleepwalker, Jonah made his way up the beach and into the forest of black and twisted trees beyond. As the roar of the bay of storms faded behind him, another sound replaced it, a strident voice that was somehow familiar in the way it pierced and clawed at his ears. It was interspersed with a chorus of hisses that raised goosebumps on his arms. He could not make out the source of the sounds, for the trees ahead tangled his view.

Jonah stumbled among the roots that rose above the black soil like broken fingers. He was soon panting, but each breath was so heavy with the stench of excrement that he could hardly take it into his lungs. As he walked, the smell grew stronger, as did the hissing and the voice, which had now reached a screaming, incoherent pitch. Then, just as he was about to clap his hands over his ears and throw up, the voice stopped, the trees thinned and Jonah saw a clearing crowded with winged, horned creatures. At their centre squatted an immense baobab tree, and before it, wrapped in a cloak, stood the source of that voice – Mr. Geist.

As Jonah appeared at the edge of the clearing, Geist raised one clawed hand. The Djinn fell silent, and turned their heads to follow his gaze. Seeing Jonah, they began hissing again, their hostility rising until it filled Jonah's head and invaded his muscles, making them twitch.

"Well, Master Jonah," Geist said. At his voice, the Djinn's hissing died. "I suppose it may be worth asking again – what will you do to free your father?"

Jonah could barely get a reply from his closed throat.

"Anything."

"Ah, that famous resolve, though not perhaps as resolved as it once was," the Elder sneered. "It seems that suffering does provide perspective. Perhaps you should have considered my initial offer of the Chant a little more carefully. Oh well, we move on. However, I can still be of assistance to you…"

Jonah narrowed his eyes. "You want to help me?"

"Of course!" Geist cried, spreading his arm magnanimously. "Why do you think I have not killed you before now? Because I need you, Jonah." He threw out his arm theatrically. "And to have killed you would have been a waste. I need you, just as you need me. So, tell me how I can help you."

"You can't," Jonah said, his body shivering uncontrollably.

Geist frowned with elaborate bemusement. "No? Really?"

Jonah clenched his fists to stop his voice from quivering. "No. Really."

Geist raised his eyebrows.

"Are you sure? After all, you are not really sure about a great many things. Your father's motive in coming here, for example…"

Jonah was silent. The dusk seemed to have flooded his insides with the greyness of Nihil.

"Very good." The Elder Djinn nodded. "Deliberation is the virtue of maturity. Now deliberate upon what I have to say. In there –" he gestured to the Nightmare tree, "– lies your father. He is asleep. In a moment he will begin the nightmare that he has known every night since entering our service. That nightmare will be a revelation to you, so I will allow you to enter the tree to observe it. When you have considered the full implications of your decision to rescue him, you may leave the tree and we will continue our discussion. My only desire is a solution that benefits us both."

Jonah stared at Geist. The Djinn host seemed frozen at the edge of his vision.

"What do you say, Master Jonah? Shall we be reasonable adults or impulsive children?"

Jonah did not reply, but his legs started moving, carrying him forward into the clearing, towards Geist and the Nightmare tree.

If the Elder Djinn was delighted, he restrained himself from expressing it. Instead, he dug his hands effortlessly into the tree bark and pulled the trunk open. He gestured towards the black opening and Jonah stepped inside.

The gap in the tree snapped shut like a mouth. A moment later, Jonah heard his father moan, but before he could locate him, the darkness exploded, and Jonah found himself in a large room surrounded by French doors. A sofa and two armchairs occupied the centre. At one end stood a dining table and four chairs, and a window opening into the kitchen beyond. It was night outside, the room dimly lit by a lamp in a corner, faded and out of focus, like the edge of an old photograph. He was in his parents' living room, and his father was on the sofa.

Francis Comfait was wearing rags that were no longer recognizable. A thick collar of dull metal encircled his neck. He sat with his shoulders slumped, as if weighed down by the collar. His hands were clasped between his knees, his eyes staring forward.

"Papa!"

Francis Comfait did not respond, but shivered and fiddled with his wedding ring. Jonah realized that his father could not see him in the dream.

A tap on the front door jerked Francis Comfait's head up, his eyes filling with anticipation and fear. Mr Geist's death's head face smiled, and he waved with mock coyness as Francis Comfait ran to open to the door.

"You were supposed to be here at eleven," Jonah's father hissed anxiously, as Geist sailed in.

"I had business elsewhere. In my line of work…"

"Yes, yes. So you've told me. Come in."

"Very kind of you. I could do with a whisky, if you have one." Geist made himself comfortable in an armchair. Francis hurried to a cabinet by the dining table. With shaking hands and a clinking of glass, he poured the drink.

Geist sipped and nodded his approval.

"You have the touch, my boy. You seem to know exactly what a tourist wants."

"I know what *you* want," Francis Comfait muttered, perching himself on the edge of a chair. "I ask for a little help and you want slavery as payment."

"Come, come, Francis," Geist said softly, spreading his arms. "That is unfair. After all, it is you who have the need. I have the means to meet that need. All I ask is a fair price."

Francis Comfait stood up abruptly and went to the cabinet, where he scrubbed a wet spot with a cloth. "You ask me to leave my family without telling them. You demand I become your slave, doing goodness knows what for goodness knows how long. And that is fair?"

"My dear man. You accumulated a lifetime of debt looking for what I have to offer. You never did tell your family exactly why you almost bankrupted them, did you? Was *that* fair?"

Francis Comfait continued wiping, though the offending spot had long since vanished.

Geist nodded with satisfaction and continued. "You never told them how obsessed you had become with finding a treasure no one else could find. That foolish notion stuck in your mind like a burr in a coat, itching you. You gave up a perfectly lucrative career in law to become a tour operator, about which you knew nothing, just so you could pursue your fantasy...

"For a while, by sheer luck, you broke even, hopeless as you were. Then there was that little political upset in your world. A few people died, and some disappeared, and then those nice men from the Ministry of Tourism came and offered to purchase your company.

"It was a good offer, but you were foolish. You held on, thinking that any day you would find what you were looking for. Your wife could stop worrying and your son would never lack for anything, and you would be free. When the government cancelled your permits and killed your business, you invented bogus tours with phantom tourists, so you could explore just one more island. And what about the costs of those expeditions? You just went on digging yourself deeper and deeper until you almost buried yourself and your family..."

Francis Comfait swept the whole counter with the cloth, as if trying to erase Geist's words, but Geist showed no signs of stopping.

"And here I offer you everything," said the Djinn, spreading his arms and smiling with all his teeth. "Not just Hodoul's measly treasure, but the wealth of kings gathered from the corners of the earth – as much as you can carry, enough to pay off your debts and ensure your family's happiness and security forever. Yet you accuse me of being unfair! What did you expect to pay for such a prize? Yes, you may have to leave your family for awhile, but only for awhile, for their good and for your peace of mind."

"So it is good that I leave my family?" Francis croaked, pacing and adjusting knick-knacks on the shelves.

"Not in the short term, no. But there is a greater good here. You could turn down my offer and be humiliated for ruining yourself and your family, with no thanks for your loyalty. Or you can make this sacrifice now for their gratitude and happiness later."

Francis looked at Geist for the first time. "But you won't even tell me when I can return to them!"

"That is because it varies from person to person…"

"It may be years. My son may have grown up. Elizabeth might have remarried!"

"Yes. It is a risk you must take. You told me, Francis, that you would be willing to give everything for your dream. Are you unwilling to test your convictions? Aren't you willing to prove yourself?"

Jonah's father was silent, then looked down.

"You see?" Geist declared. "You want to do it! Yet when I give you the opportunity you accuse me of trying to rob you of your life."

"I wasn't accusing you."

"Really? It certainly sounded like it to me!"

"It's just that…"

"Now you listen to me, Monsieur Francis Comfait." Geist's voice was suddenly piercing and cold. "I do not have time for dithering. I am a businessman and I am making you an offer. You can have what you have almost ruined yourself to find, for my price, or I can leave your home right now. It is a simple choice."

Francis Comfait began to fiddle with his wedding ring again. Beads of sweat had broken out on his forehead. "I can't..." he said. "Just like that..."

"Then I will make it easy. In five seconds, I will leave your home. I will not return."

Francis's eyes beseeched Geist, who returned his gaze expressionlessly.

"Goodbye, my dear boy," Geist said, standing and turning towards the door.

"No, stop," Francis Comfait said, reaching out to Geist, "I agree."

"Fine," he said without emotion. "Take it." He held out the pendant that Jonah recognized as the one he had been offered.

Francis Comfait stared at the rock, then reached out a shaking hand, his fingers not quite touching it.

"You have to take it," Geist said. "I cannot put it in your hand."

"One thing first."

"What now?"

"I can't... They can't think that I just left."

"So?" Geist asked coldly.

"Can't we make it that I was lost somehow?"

"Lost how?"

"Lost at sea, perhaps..."

"I am not playing games, Francis." Geist took a step towards the door.

"No, Geist! I want it! You know how much! I just want this one... allowance."

Geist paused, weighing the implications. "It seems complicated," he concluded.

"No, no," Francis Comfait's hands fluttered over one another. "We can take my boat. I register you as a guest. We abandon her on the open ocean, perhaps in a storm. What else can they think?"

"How long will this take?"

"A week to get her out of the shipping lanes. That's all I'm asking."

"Fine," Geist said. "Now take the pendant."

Francis took a deep breath, and clutched at the rock with sudden force.

"Put it on."

Francis put the pendant over his head. He did not seem to notice the lead collar he was already wearing.

"Let's go to your ship."

Geist walked into the night. Jonah's father stood for a moment in the doorway, and looked around the room. His eyes were desolate, but when he realized that Geist was no longer nearby, he shivered abruptly, turned and vanished into the night.

The room faded, leaving the pitch darkness of the Nightmare tree, and the echoing of sobs.

Chapter 20

THE GREAT DEFEAT

Jonah was overwhelmed by the smell — the acrid excrement of Nihil combined with his father's odour of sweat and filth, of fear and despair. He fell on his knees and threw up, until his throat was burning with bile. When there was nothing but spasms, he found himself unable to move. All he could do was listen to his father's moans nearby.

"Would you like to forget this?" Jonah looked around. Geist's head, glowing faintly, seemed to be floating.

"No child should see his father like this," Geist continued. "Every child should remember their father well."

"I can't —" Jonah tried to speak, but the words clawed at his throat.

"There are powers you cannot conceive of, Jonah. I can help you to forget. More than that, I can help you to remember your father as he should be, as he once was, perhaps.

"Give yourself to us, Jonah. Give yourself and I will give you a dream unlike anything you have ever known. Your mother will adore you, your father will always be there to go sailing with you. You will inherit his ship and be successful in everything you do. You will have the love of a beautiful woman, adoring children. And you will die at a hundred, surrounded by your grandchildren."

"But I would really be here."

"You would. But why care about reality when you can have something better?"

"And what about my…" Jonah hesitated. "What about him?"

"He is almost used up. You know what that means, so you know he will very soon no longer be your father."

Jonah closed his eyes to block out the Djinn's face, but that pale, bald head floated in his mind. He realized now that his horror was not shock. It was knowing that his worst fears had come true. Somewhere inside, since his first night on Captain Aquille's island, he had known why his father had gone with the Djinn. He had known that he had not been tricked.

Suddenly, Jonah longed to forget. It would be easy for Geist to do. After all, what was left of the man he had called his father? And the more he chased the question, the farther away the answers blew.

Somehow Monvieil had foreseen all this. So why, *why*, had he sent Jonah here?

Whatever you lose, Monvieil had said, *remember how Tinashe triumphed…* A love like hers would open the prison. But was there anything left to love?

"I want to speak to him," Jonah said. "Before I do anything."

Geist's eyes narrowed. "Take my word for it. He has nothing to say."

"I don't care. I won't give anything until I'm sure you are right."

"Very well. Talk to him."

"Without the collar."

Geist's head jerked.

"He can talk with the collar on!"

"I want him *free* to talk."

"Fine then!"

Jonah felt Geist's cloak brush past. He followed the Elder deeper into the tree. Then Geist was bending forward, and Jonah discerned his father's outline in the glow from the Elder's head.

"Leave me alone!" Francis shouted, writhing at the Djinn's touch.

"Hold still, you fool! I am taking off the collar!"

"Leave me alone!"

Then there was a sharp *click*, and Francis sighed and was quiet.

"There," Geist said. "My offer expires in three minutes." He disappeared.

Jonah knelt beside his father. He tried to say, "Papa," but the sound died in his throat.

"Who are you?" Francis asked.

"I am Jonah." Then he made himself say it – "Your son."

"My son. A good boy, that one."

"Papa." Jonah reached out a shaking hand and touched his father's shoulder. "I'm here."

"You came a long way, my son."

"Yes I did."

"You learned to sail on the ocean. Well done!" Francis yawned.

Anger flashed into Jonah's throat. "I know everything, Papa. I know what you did."

His father was silent.

"I learned how to sail a long time ago," Francis said finally. "But I never got really good. Not like you."

"Papa…"

"I'm sorry, my boy. I am so sorry."

"That's not good enough." Jonah's voice shivered with anger and tears.

"I know." Jonah felt his father's hand on his arm, and pulled away.

"I'm almost used up now, Jonah. Time for you to go home."

Jonah rose to his feet. "Yes," he said. "Time to go home." He turned away from his father and felt his way towards the trunk.

"Jonah."

Jonah stopped, but did not turn back.

"Tell your mother about me. Ask her to forgive me."

"I never told her I was going, Papa. I never trusted her either…"

"Don't compare yourself to me! You left selflessly. I left for myself only."

Jonah said nothing.

"Promise that you will ask her to forgive me one more time."

Suddenly, something seemed to give way in Jonah's chest. He knew at last what he had to do.

"I promise," he whispered.

"You learned to sail on the ocean. Just remember that. You learned how to sail on the ocean by yourself."

Jonah knocked on the tree trunk, and it split apart, revealing Geist and the host of the Djinn behind him.

"What is your answer?" Geist said, his eyeholes boring into Jonah.

"I don't want to forget anything."

"So?" Geist hissed.

Jonah took a deep breath. "Let him go. Send him back to Monvieil. I will stay. No dreams, just reality."

There was a silence.

"No benefits?" Geist said incredulously. "Are you insane, boy?"

"I must be," Jonah said. "But that's what I want."

"You'll wear the collar and live your worst nightmares…"

"Yes."

"For the rest of your life."

"Yes."

Geist looked back at the Djinn as if to confirm what he had heard. They were mute with confusion. Only Malach felt defeat and death descending to crush him.

Geist turned back to Jonah, an amused expression on his face. "How nobly foolish! And for a moment I thought you were worthy to be my enemy. Very well, you have your wish." He held up the collar. "Come forward."

Jonah obeyed and Geist slipped the collar around his neck, locking it so tightly that the metal bit into his flesh. Jonah winced at the pain, but forgot it almost immediately as the world went dark and a wave of nausea overcame him. Everything spun around him, light and darkness. When the spinning slowed, outlines of trees at the edge of the clearing, the sky, Geist and the host behind him – all had disappeared into a grey blur.

A claw clamped painfully on his shoulder and Jonah was dragged backwards into the tree and hurled to the ground. The collar had grown insupportable; he could not lift his head from the stinking earth.

"You can begin your slavery at once. You, Comfait!" Geist shouted at Jonah's father, his voice distant and distorted. "Get up! You should be proud. Your son has bought your freedom!"

"What do you mean?" Francis said, his voice so faint that Jonah could barely hear it.

"You're going, he's staying. Get up!"

"Jonah, I forbid it!" his father shouted. "I'm still your father, and I forbid it!"

"I said, get up!" snarled Geist.

Francis screamed, but the screams and shouts faded into a distant roar, like the sound of the sea in a conch. Geist closed the Nightmare tree.

Jonah dropped into an abyss in the centre of his mind, as if he was collapsing inwards. He moaned and reached out to stop himself, but his hands were gone. He was floating disembodied over an vast emptiness. Then a wind, like the beginning of the new monsoon, blew in his face. The darkness receded before the wind, fading, fading...

Chapter 21

THE GREATER DEFEAT

He was sailing his dinghy *Albatross* across a still ocean. His father was running beside him on the water, encouraging him; but Jonah could not understand his words. Then the boat capsized and Jonah was in the water, drifting down through the sunbeams towards the ocean floor far below. Jonah looked up to see his father still standing on the ocean, looking down and smiling like a pirate with treasure.

Jonah's chest ached from lack of breath. Then he coughed, and seawater flooded his nose and mouth. As his last breath bubbled from his lips, his struggle weakened. Then he knew he had died, and he was gliding like a seagull on outstretched wings. And in death, he could see the ocean floor spread out beneath him like an endless moonlit wasteland.

Empty as death.

Except there was something standing on that dead plain. As

Jonah descended, he saw that it was a house with a minaret roof. But it was too small for a house…

No, it was an Angelus Lamp.

Then he was alive again, breathing water like air. He reached down and grasped the lamp by its handle. He was rushing up towards the surface, carried on an endless breath of bubbles.

He broke the surface, and then he was standing on the water and his parents were sitting at his feet, holding each other like frightened children and looking up at the sky. He followed their desolate gazes and saw Geist descending from the clouds on outspread wings, a drawn scimitar outstretched in his hand, leading the Djinn like a horde of locusts.

The lamp floated before Jonah in the wind. He reached out and took it, thinking how light it was in a dream. And as if every movement had been predicted since the beginning, he held the lamp up towards the descending Djinn, crying out in a voice that shook the mountain beneath him, ONE FILLING ALL, LIFT ME FOREVER TO YOU!

Outside the Nightmare tree, Geist faced the Djinn host.

"Soon," the Elder said quietly, "we will feast."

The frenzied host hissed and danced up and down.

"But before then, we have a little justice to dispense…"

The Djinn snickered in anticipation.

"Malach! Bagat! Traitors! Turn and face your brothers!"

Bagat hung his head, but Malach stared defiantly.

"Here is what happens to those who disobey the Elder and betray their family!" And with what seemed like no effort, Geist slashed at Bagat's neck. Bagat opened his mouth to scream, but no sound came out. Instead, his severed head bounced sideways and crunched on the sand, blood spurting from his neck. Then Geist was on top of the body, slashing, tearing, as blood splattered his face and cloak until Bagat the Djinn was a mere heap of shredded flesh and bones.

Well, Malach thought dryly, *there goes a perfectly good apprentice.*

The Elder wiped the blood from his face with his cloak. He swept his gaze over the host, but no one looked up. Then he glanced at Malach, who was staring straight ahead with defiance etched in every line of his skeletal face.

"I have kept the best until last," Geist whispered to him. Then, loudly, "With this, our justice is complete!" And he raised his claw.

But as his stroke descended, a Djinn cried out, "The Tree is burning!"

The Elder spun around. The branches that had put forth small, spear-shaped leaves and bunches of black fruit were smoking, then bursting into blue flame. Within seconds, the whole tree was consumed in a fire whose colour and intensity the Elder Djinn remembered only too clearly. Years before, the lone figure of a man stood on the peak of a mountain, holding up a lamp. The fire had rolled towards Geist like a breaking wave, reducing him to ashes. He remembered the agony of that defeat and the painstaking years in Chaos before his return to Mysterion. The Elder remembered all these things, and felt a rock-slide of disaster descending again as he watched Wind-Fire engulf his beloved tree.

While the Elder was occupied with his nightmare, Malach had slipped out reach, sidled up to one of his brother Djinn and slipped his scimitar from its sheath. Before he could challenge the Elder, however, the flames surrounding the Nightmare tree parted to let through a slight figure who walked as if in a dream.

Jonah felt the flames burning through him, eating through his heart and mind until they were emptied of everything but the certainty that he had accomplished the triumph of Tinashe again. Then he was awake. The burning tree stood behind him now, but he could still see the flames of Wind-Fire rippling over his skin, though they no longer caused him pain. Instead he felt protected, enveloped in a vast sense of serenity.

Confronted by Wind-Fire in the form of the boy who had eluded him so long, Geist shrieked, "I don't know what trick you used for this, boy, but you will never defeat *me!*" And he flew at Jonah's throat with both claws extended.

Then Malach flew up behind the Elder, and his scimitar whispered in the air. The Elder's eyeholes widened as his head fell from his body. From full flight, he flopped onto the sand. Malach hacked up the Elder as quickly as the Elder had mauled Bagat. Finally, he pulled the bloody cloak from the Elder's corpse and draped it around himself. Jonah braced himself, expecting Malach to continue the Elder's attack, but the Djinn only felt around in the cloak and pulled out the pendant that the Elder had offered to Jonah so long ago. Then he attempted to wink grotesquely.

"Couldn't let him ruin a nice warm cloak." He grinned. "And a stunning piece of jewellery to match!"

He turned his back on Jonah and faced the host, frozen by shock at seeing the Nightmare tree destroyed and then Jonah appearing from the flames. Being creatures of short memory, they had long ago forgotten Malach's plan, or had dismissed it as too foolhardy against one as powerful as the Elder. Seeing Geist cut down now threw them into a kind of madness. They milled aimlessly, hissing and shouting, fearful and accusing.

Then Malach raised his claw and they instinctively fell silent before the authority of the cloak and pendant.

"My brothers!" He shouted. "We are free!"

The host shifted and muttered.

"From now on, we will answer to no one but ourselves! Free, brothers, and equal!" He paused to let his words sink in. "Our brother Bagat died at the hands of the tyrant Geist!" He gestured at the piles of bloody flesh and bones by his feet. He sensed that the mood was shifting, like the changing of the monsoon. Just a little push… "Do not let his sacrifice go in vain!"

Not quite enough, Malach thought. *Who cared about sacrifice?*

As he furiously searched his mind for something to galvanize them, the solution arrived. The Wind-Fire had left the Nightmare tree in ashes and spread outwards like wings to consume the surrounding trees. Now it twisted upwards, burning off the clouds that cloaked Nihil, and the late afternoon sun of Mysterion showered down on Jonah and the Djinn. Pierced by the light, the Djinn whimpered and tried to hide. Only Jonah gratefully raised his face to the sky. Then he smiled, and the last of Nihil's darkness blew from his heart.

"Angeli," he whispered.

And, indeed, the sky was full of brilliant, fluttering figures bearing swords, descending rank on rank from the East.

Malach, attempting to conceal himself from the light with his cloak, squinted upwards, his expression freezing in horror. But he hesitated only for a moment. He drew himself up and gestured at the clear sky and the Wind-Fire.

"Brothers!" he shouted. "You must now choose! You can stay and face the Fire and the Angeli, who even now are upon us! Or you can follow me into the West and regain your strength!"

The Djinn looked up and broke out into an ululation of terror. The sight of the Angeli hosts robbed them of their last uncertainties.

"We are with you, Father!"

"Save us, Elder Brother!"

Malach pointed to where the sky was turning bloody as the sun descended towards it. "To the West!" He glanced at Jonah.

"We will meet again, Master Jonah. Perhaps you will remember my mercy to you." And he rose into the air, collapsing into the form of a bluebottle fly. The rest of the Djinn followed, until what remained of the burning island − a bare patch of black dirt burning to ash − swarmed with flies. They swarmed Jonah, then formed themselves into a rough arrowhead and darted up towards the West, vanishing into the sunset.

The Angeli were approaching now; Jonah was able to make out the leader, holding her sword before her, smiling at him with that familiar sarcastic smile, and joy overwhelmed him.

"Azrel!" he shouted, waving wildly. "Azrel! Here I am!"

Chapter 22

THE INHERITANCE GIVEN

They flew all night. Jonah on Azrel's back, too excited to sleep. His mind was so full of questions that for once he didn't mind the amused tone in which she answered, as if he was a small child.

"When we realized that we weren't going to make the Cyclops let you go, we were in a bit of a state as we turned back. But of course Monvieil had seen us in the Pools and sent the Angeli to meet us. We returned and found the Cyclops in a unbelievable rage, but finally got him to calm down and learned that you had gotten away. So we flew to where the smoke of Nihil began and waited. The Djinn magic prevented us from pushing through the reef of fire. Pretty frustrating, but there wasn't much else we could do."

"I'm sorry," Jonah said.

"I wasn't too worried." Azrel grinned, "The Djinn wouldn't care about a shrimp like you."

"Your flattery is touching."

"But wasn't I right? You did fine, didn't you?"

Jonah thought of Geist flying towards him, wings spread and face white and staring. He shivered. "Yes," he said quietly. "I did."

Azrel, too, became serious. "Monvieil told me that all would be well if you remembered Tinashe. I didn't know exactly what he meant, but when I saw the Wind-Fire clearing the fog, I knew that he had been right." She was silent a moment. "It's good to see you alive."

"It was good to see you too." *So Monvieil had known, in a way at least…*

They were silent as Jonah stared over the moonlit sea, broken into infinite reflections. As they passed over the island of pirates, Jonah could just make out the bonfires on the beaches. He thought about Sartish and was sad, but instinctively kept himself from telling Azrel about the pirate boy. Somehow that memory seemed better tucked away.

"Will the pirates ever be free?"

"There's always hope of freedom in Mysterion."

"The Djinn will be back," he said. "Malach said we would meet again."

"They will always come back. Until the higher Mysterion comes."

"When?"

"No one knows. Not even Monvieil."

"Perhaps never, then…"

"Not never!" Azrel insisted. "In time. Until then, we struggle on."

"Is my father all right?"

"We found him adrift in a boat on the edge of Nihil. He is with Monvieil."

"But is he all right?"

"He wouldn't stop weeping. He kept on crying that he didn't want you to stay. If we hadn't forced him to go with us, he would have killed himself trying to get back through the reef of fire."

Jonah closed his eyes. He remembered the sensation of falling inside himself when Geist had closed him in the Nightmare Tree. That abyss would always be there. But so would the wind. There was always the Wind.

"Are you all right?"

Jonah opened his eyes to see Azrel looking back at him in concern.

"I feel old," he said, smiling lopsidedly. "Older than my own father."

Azrel nodded. "Because you live in Mysterion now. And Mysterion is older than all time that you have known. Besides," she smiled, "you have to be older if you are going to be an Elder."

"What?" Jonah frowned.

"Monvieil will explain. Rest now."

Suddenly, exhaustion collapsed on him like a landslide, and he laid his head on Azrel's fluttering shoulders.

Jonah woke to the softness of a bed and a vision of butterfly children floating and swirling above him. Occasionally two or three darted close to giggle into his face before dancing away. He sat up, and the butterfly children parted, screaming with excitement. He was lying in the bower where he had slept the first night in Mysterion. Beyond the open doorway was Monvieil's garden. A pair of unicorns grazed nearby; the Seeing Pools glinted among the trees in the distance.

Then a hand gripped his shoulder. His father was squatting beside him, his face pale and haggard, his eyes underlined by lack of sleep – the way Jonah's mother had looked for days after he had left.

His father held out his hand, overflowing with Bright fruit gathered from the garden. "Breakfast," he said.

The fruit was delicious, and when he had finished, Jonah felt strong and alert.

"I didn't want that to happen to you, Jonah," Francis said.

"I know," Jonah said, meeting his eyes with a smile. "But don't worry. From now on I'll try to do what you want. Most of the time." His smiled broadened into a grin.

His father did not return the smile. "I don't know why you would."

"You are my father," Jonah replied. "And you taught me to sail. Speaking of which, I crossed the reef at home in *Albatross*. She's not bad on the open water, you know."

"Really?" The trace of a smile infused Francis's face.

"I sailed her all the way to Captain Aquille's island."

"Tell me," he said.

Later that morning, they walked together to where Monvieil lay. The old man had grown very frail, his features blurred with pain. Azrel and King Nicholas stood behind the couch. Azrel greeted Jonah with a smile and King Nicholas tossed his mane. With an effort, the old man gestured them forward. Jonah and his father knelt down to hear his words.

"So, my boy," Monvieil whispered. "Are you done?"

"Yes, Sire."

"Good. That's good. Now what do you want to know?"

Jonah sighed with relief. There were two questions that Azrel could not answer.

"Why didn't I stay in the nightmare?"

"Only those who sell themselves to the Djinn are imprisoned by them. Geist thought he was getting a free slave, but what he failed to understand was that there is no such thing. A slave is *always* paid for. So when you *gave* yourself, his tree failed to imprison you with that drowning nightmare. Instead you were free to dream that you were like Tinashe, giving yourself for the life of others."

Jonah hesitated, his mind overwhelmed.

"One more, Sire," he said at last. "Did you know what would happen from the very beginning?"

Monvieil smiled.

"I knew you were willing to follow where the Wind blew. That was enough. Now it is time for you to return home to your mother and your life in Lethes. It is also time for me to do what I have longed to do – return to the Wind."

Azrel pursed her lips.

"As you can see," Monvieil continued, glancing up at Azrel, "I have no more strength for this task. I am leaving Azrel and King Nicholas as regents until you return to take up the throne."

Jonah stared. "Me?"

"Of course. You have shown yourself willing to follow the Wind. You are worthy of this inheritance. Of course, there is growing up still to be done, but when the time comes, you can continue the work that I, that is, Captain Aquille, started." Azrel reached behind the couch and brought out the Angelus Lamp that Jonah had lost.

"Where did you find it?" he cried.

"The mermaids found it at the bottom of the sea, where the Cyclops tossed it," Monvieil answered. "It is yours again, to use when you are old enough, as I once used it. Lead the Letheis back to Mysterion. It will be a slow process, one person at a time, but in time they will return to real life – or join the pirates – and then the higher Mysterion will begin."

Azrel held out the lamp. Tentatively, Jonah took it.

"But how do I teach them?"

"Don't worry," Monvieil assured him. "You will find a way. Your way. Do not try to repeat what Captain Aquille did. He had his ways and yours will come to you in time. Until then, put the lamp away. When the time is right, the Wind will lead you to it and you will know what to do. Now it is time to go. Azrel, have them bring the bier."

Azrel signalled and four Angeli carrying a wooden platform piled with purple cushions floated out of the trees. Gently they lifted the old man onto it. When he was settled, he gestured to Jonah and his father.

"I want to show you one last thing before we go."

The escort moved into the trees. King Nicholas walked beside the bier at a dignified pace, while Jonah and his father followed behind. The butterfly children, anticipating some new game, brought up the rear like bright leaves swirling on in the wind. As the trees thinned, they emerged onto a plateau bathed in golden sunlight. They stopped at the far side, where the plateau dropped away down a sharp, scrub-covered slope to a forest. As far as Jonah could see, the land below the cliff was filled with people. Men and women of all ages and varieties, children darting around among them, all looked up towards them, and when Monvieil raised his hand in greeting, they sent out a great cheer.

"Long live Monvieil!" they shouted. "Long live the Elder!"

At last, their cheers subsided and Monvieil spoke. He did not talk loudly, yet his voice seemed to resound inside Jonah's head. The crowd must have heard him the same way, because now even the children were still, looking up at the frail figure on the bier.

"My children," he said. "As you know, I must leave you today."

The silence persisted, but Jonah could feel the palpable grief of the people.

"As you also have known," Monvieil continued. "You will be well guarded by the Angeli, whose commander you all know. The Cyclops defends your border. You will be safe from the pirates."

The people murmured their appreciation and a cheer went up.

"But there is more. One day, you will have a new Elder, one who is even now standing before you." Monvieil pointed to Jonah. "You have heard his name and you have learned how he has cast out the Djinn from our realm." Monvieil grasped Jonah's hand and raised it. "He is worthy!"

"He is worthy!" the people roared in reply.

"He is worthy!" The old man's voice boomed in Jonah's head.

The people echoed the cry.

"He is worthy!" Monvieil's voice penetrated his heart.

"He is worthy!" the people affirmed.

"But he is young yet," Monvieil said. "And so he must return to Lethes until his years have ripened. Until then, I bequeath him the name of Elder, which he has earned in action, if not in years."

The people cheered.

"And now it is time for homecomings." Monvieil looked at Jonah, who nodded. Only Francis Comfait looked pale. He opened his mouth, then closed it.

"Yes, Francis?" Monvieil said. "What do you want to know?"

"Forgive me, Highness," Francis Comfait stuttered. "Will I...forget all this? Afterwards?" Francis Comfait swept his hand to encompass all Mysterion.

"Not at first," Monvieil replied. "But when you awake in Lethes, you will decide not to tell anyone what you have seen. The world will be amazed at your reappearance, but they will credit it to your superior survival skills and the tenacity of your son, and you will agree. In time, you will start to think that you dreamed it all. You will find ways to explain everything, and what does not fit you will ignore, with the help of Lethes."

"Oh." Jonah's father looked down.

"Your sorrow will pass. You are of the Letheis, and it is the way of the Letheis to forget."

"But I want to remember."

"Then you must learn how to remember truly," the old man said. "Perhaps one day, Jonah will teach you and you can return to Mysterion and find this memory again."

"So *I* will remember?" Jonah asked.

"Yes. Unlike Captain Aquille, you will be blessed – or cursed – to remember this time of waking in the middle of your Letheis dream. Blessed because you will gain strength from your memories. Cursed because you will have to conceal your true self."

"Conceal?" Jonah frowned. "From whom?"

"Letheis do not believe in Mysterion, and they will hate you for believing. You must learn to whom you can safely reveal your knowledge. Not everyone can be trusted with the secrets of Mysterion. They can be found only by those who have the right heart to look for them. Do you understand?"

"Not really." Jonah shook his head.

"You will one day. Now, are you ready?"

Jonah nodded.

"And you, Francis?"

Jonah's father nodded.

"Jonah, hold out the lamp. Francis, touch the surface. Do not let go. Just as the lamp was a door into Mysterion, so it will return you to the place in Lethes where it was last kindled. You can find your way home from there."

He raised his head to address the people below.

"Farewell, my children!" he called. The silence that had covered the whole island until that moment now broke as an elderly woman in the crowd wept. The sound carried clearly up to the plateau and Jonah felt tears fill his eyes.

"Goodbye Jonah," Azrel called.

He turned and met her gaze, but could not reply.

She grinned. "And grow some muscle before you return. I can't keep doing all the hard work!"

Jonah stuck out his tongue at her, and Francis Comfait laughed for the first time.

Monvieil shook his head in mock exasperation. "Very well, very well. Now Jonah, Francis — focus, both of you."

They fixed their attention on the glittering surface where fishermen cast their nets and Angeli flew eternally. Monvieil blew on the wick as if extinguishing its invisible flame. As he did so, a wind sprung up and blew around them in circles. Below, the sounds of weeping had intensified. As the wind circled faster, kicking up earth and leaves, a young man cried out: "Long live Monvieil! Long live the new Elder of Mysterion!"

As the wind picked up strength, the outlines of Monvieil's face blurred; then his body dissolved like a sand sculpture. The light, first dulled by debris, failed completely. Azrel, the Angeli, King Nicholas − the whole of Mysterion − vanished. For an instant, Jonah saw the faint image of an old man's face, smiling. Then that too was gone. He felt himself dissolving in the storm, spiralling down through the darkness. A moment later, the storm parted and he was falling slowly, his father beside him. It was getting brighter, as only dust covered the sun, obscuring its brightness. Daylight.

Jonah saw a limitless ocean below him, dull blue, and an island. Closer now, there was a beach and his own body collapsed on the sand above the high-tide mark. His father's body lay half in and half out of the water, bobbing slightly as the waves broke over him. Then he was rushing down at himself and darkness flooded through his head.

Chapter 23

THE RETURN

The Coast Guard vessel motored out of the sunrise, towards the harbour. Jonah and his father stood at the aft rail, the cool breeze ruffling their hair. Pirogues overflowing with the night's catch overtook them, heading to the beach where the housewives waited with empty baskets.

Ahead, Jonah could see the dock with its cluster of white buildings amid a forest of yacht masts. Behind sprawled the town: tin-roofed buildings, stone churches and bright shacks, climbing partway up the mountain, which rose, thick with forests, to massive granite peaks. The sight was beautiful, but also sad.

Jonah sighed.

His father glanced sideways and smiled. "It's good to be back."

"Yes," Jonah said. He knew his father would not understand his sadness.

"I've been thinking," Francis said, after a pause. "Maybe it would be best to keep our adventures to ourselves. I mean, just for a while. Somehow I survived the storm that wrecked my boat. The current carried me to Aquille's island. You ran away and hid because you were afraid to get in trouble for running away to rescue me… something like that. It's not strictly speaking true, I know," his father said. "But I think it will be for the greater good."

Tears filled Jonah's eyes. Monvieil had been right. This was the way of Lethes.

"Just for a while," his father repeated. "Until things calm down."

"All right," Jonah sighed, staring at the green water swirling and creaming against the side of the ship.

"Are you sure?"

"What about Maman?"

Francis Comfait started to shake his head, but something in Jonah's expression made him change his mind. "We…" he hesitated. "We could probably tell her…"

"Yes," Jonah said. "I think that would be right."

Francis nodded and lowered his gaze. Jonah looked back to where Captain Aquille's island was sharply outlined in the morning sun.

They had awakened on the island, where Jonah had kindled the lamp. Captain Aquille had disappeared. In his house they had discovered an envelope containing a notarized will in which he gave the island and everything on it to Jonah, to be held in trust until he came of age.

They were approaching the dock now. Jonah could see his mother, wearing a yellow chiffon dress. *Her Saturday dress,* he thought, and smiled. Behind her a crowd gathered – friends, relatives and the usual hangers on and loiterers. The only discordant note was the group of Tanzanian soldiers gathered near the harbourmaster's office, leaning on the railings with their customary boredom.

As the boat bumped gently against the pylons, Francis waved above his head and the crowd cheered. A woman was taking pictures near a man writing on a notepad. Tomorrow, his father's version of their story would be in the newspaper, but this was of no interest to Jonah. He was feeling the first trace of a muted joy, the joy of seeing his mother again, knowing that he could tell the truth and that somehow she would understand.

As soon as the gangplank clattered onto the dock, Francis Comfait ran down and embraced his wife. Jonah followed amid applause and cheering and the clicking of cameras. His mother reached out and pulled him into the embrace.

Then she leaned away.

"You two stink," she said, wrinkling her nose.

Francis raised his arm and sniffed. "It has been a while." And he smiled.

Then Elizabeth was crying without a sound, one tear following the other slowly down her cheeks.

"I'm sorry, Elizabeth," Francis whispered, reaching out and stroking her cheek.

"It's all gone," she said. "I sold to Harry, but they got to him too – they took everything."

Francis glanced up at the soldiers.

"It's all right. Things will change, and we'll begin again."

Elizabeth Comfait did not reply. Her tears were coming faster now. She pulled Jonah close.

He could smell the eternal lilacs in her perfume. "I'm sorry too, Maman."

"I knew it would be today," she murmured. "Today, I would know about you for certain. Either way. I insisted that Monsieur Joubert send the Coast Guard west with the monsoon. I told him that they would find you." She was smiling through her tears now.

Jonah knew the answer, but he had to ask anyway: "How did you know, Maman?"

"I had a dream one night. A very strange dream about an island more beautiful even than this one. I dreamed about strange people covered with wings and trees with diamonds for fruits and butterflies with children's faces and lions and unicorns. And there was a man – his face was too bright for me to see – and he told me things I could not understand. But when I woke up, I was certain that today would be the end of the story."

"Strange how dreams can be," Francis Comfait said. He glanced around at the crowd, but no one seemed to be listening. They were chatting loudly and bottles of beer had appeared from nowhere. Even the soldiers, their interest finally piqued, were sauntering down to demand a bottle.

Jonah met his mother's eyes and smiled.

"Let's go home," he said. "I'll tell you the rest."

Epilogue

THE HIDDEN ISLANDS
ARE HERE

Jonah walked down to the beach in the early morning, carrying the Angelus Lamp. The sun was rising in his face, the water calm out to the reef. Jonah made his way along the beach to a large takamaka tree near the rocks.

At the tree's base, he rolled aside a round granite boulder, exposing a hollow, and pulled out a catapult and bow and arrows, a model sailboat, a tangle of fishing line, a hook and a bait tin. Into the space, he slipped the lamp and concealed the hollow again. He gathered up his old toys and walked back towards the head of the beach and the sea road.

When he arrived home, the lights were on. His father's head appeared in the upstairs window. Jonah tried to catch his eye with a wave, but Francis Comfait did not see him in the darkness. He disappeared from view.

Jonah paused at the front door. Early shadows filled the garden. In the mango trees, crickets chirruped and doves cooed in the tapping of coconut fronds, and he thought he heard a familiar refrain somewhere in that cacophony: "Long live Monvieil! Long live the Elder of Mysterion!"

Jonah listened. Then he smiled, clutched his old toys closer and exhaled a single breath.

"The Hidden Islands are here," he whispered. And he stepped inside.

A Note About the Setting of this Book

The Seychelles is a nation comprised of islands north of Madagascar and east of Kenya. Archaeological evidence suggests that the islands were probably discovered some time in the ninth to tenth centuries by Arab sailors who stopped to bury their dead. Some sources say that they knew the archipelago as "The Land of the Djinn." Later, in the sixteenth century, the Portuguese explorer Vasco de Gama sighted the islands, which he called "the Seven Sisters," but did not approach for fear of uncharted shoals and reefs.

Apart from being used as a station to restock on water, coconuts and fresh tortoise meat, the archipelago remained uninhabited by human beings until 1770, when the French, accompanied by African slaves and East Indian merchants, formed a permanent colony. Though conquered by the British in 1794, the Seychellois people lived in peace, intermingling to form a unique Creole language and culture out of their varied European, African and Asian backgrounds. During this time, the islands became a paradise for tourists seeking unspoiled natural beauty and a warm climate. After the Seychelles was granted independence from Great Britain in 1976, political upheaval returned. The year following independence, a *coup d'état* assisted by the Tanzanian army placed a new communist-style government in control. Since then, the Seychelles has returned to democracy, and remains an exotic destination for tourists from Europe and North America. For more information, please visit the country's official web site at www.seychelles.com.

Acknowledgments

For the creation and publication of this work, I would like to extend my thanks to a number of people. First and foremost, I am eternally grateful to my long-suffering wife Jaime, who read this book more times than she wanted to... Thank you, Amanda Kits, my first young adult reader; Mary Armstrong, my first editor; Michelle Holloway, for her detailed insights. Thanks to my friend James Mullin, for opening doors; to Michael Katz, who led me through the wilderness; to the F.E. Osborne Junior High Grade 7A and 7B class of 2005-2006, for their appreciation and comments. A big thanks to the staff of Coteau Books, who were so kind, patient and professional in their dealings with me, especially Barbara Sapergia, for being the book's champion (every book needs one). Finally, I thank and embrace Charis Wahl – your sympathetic mind, and swift and elegant pencil raised this work to another level.

About the Author

Richard René is a teacher in Calgary. He is also an Eastern Orthodox priest with a congregation of diverse cultural backgrounds, including native-born Canadians, Russians, Eritreans and East Indians. As a boy growing up in the Seychelles, he experienced the rich mixture of peoples, myths and cultures there, which now find a place in his fiction. He also remembers reading Michael Ende's *The Neverending Story,* a work of marvellous invention which still inspires him as a writer. Richard and his wife have three children. *The Nightmare Tree* is his first publication.